WANTING MOR

WANTING
MOR

Rukhsana Khan

GROUNDWOOD BOOKS
HOUSE OF ANANSI PRESS
TORONTO BERKELEY

Groundwood Books / House of Anansi Press
groundwoodbooks.com

We acknowledge for their financial support of our publishing program the Canada
Council for the Arts, the Ontario Arts Council and the Government of Canada.

Canada Council   Conseil des Arts
for the Arts   du Canada

ONTARIO ARTS COUNCIL
CONSEIL DES ARTS DE L'ONTARIO
an Ontario government agency
un organisme du gouvernement de l'Ontario

With the participation of the government of Canada | Canadä
Avec la participation du gouvernement du Canada

Library and Archives Canada Cataloguing in Publication
Khan, Rukhsana
Wanting Mor / Rukhsana Khan.
ISBN 978-0-88899-858-3 (bound).–ISBN 978-0-88899-862-0 (pbk.)
1. Afghan War, 2001- –Juvenile fiction. 2. Girls–Afghanistan–Juvenile
fiction. 3. Orphanages–Afghanistan–Juvenile fiction. I. Title.
PS8571.H42W35 2009   jC813'.54   C2008-905687-6

Design by Michael Solomon
Printed and bound in Canada

MIX
Paper from
responsible sources
FSC® C004071

*To Huwa, Najibah and Karima Yousufi,
to my daughters, Ruqayyah, Hafsa and
Nusaybah Alli, and to all the women who
strive to emulate the wives of the Prophet
(peace be upon him).*

1

I THOUGHT she was sleeping. It was a relief to wake up to silence after all that coughing during the past few days.

I peeked in on her before I started the fire. I swept the floor and grabbed some ash from the fireplace. I washed the dishes without her telling me to, thinking, Won't she be pleased? Won't she rub her hand on my hair and smile at me with that look on her face that I love? The one that says she wouldn't exchange me for all the money in the world.

I scrubbed those pots until my knuckles hurt. I wanted them to gleam so that she could see her face in them.

When Baba comes home she still hasn't woken up. I take out the leftovers from last night's supper and warm them on the fire. He eats quickly and licks the bowl so clean with his finger that I hardly need to wash it.

A few grumbles and he's gone again.

I clean up, pray Zuhr and still she hasn't woken up. With the last of the buffalo milk I make her a cup of tea just the way she likes it and push open the door.

"Mor?"

I know immediately that something is wrong.

The room is too quiet. The skin on her face is too slack.

A wail escapes from me before I can stifle it. My legs are going to collapse. I sit down heavily on the edge of the charpaee. The jute ropes creak with my weight and it jostles her body.

Gently, gently. Do not disturb her. The cup feels too hot in my hands. I stare down stupidly at the milky brown liquid. There's froth at the edge of the cup, and some of the bubbles are bursting.

Am I dreaming?

My toes brush the mud floor of our hut. The trampled dirt is soft against my rough feet. I slowly look back at my mother.

She's dead.

Should I try to revive her? I put down the cup and grab her hand. Stiff and cold! I drop it like it burned me. "Inna lillahi wa inna ilaihi rajioon." Rocking back and forth, over and over I repeat the words, "Inna lillahi wa inna ilaihi rajioon." Indeed from God we have come and to Him is our return.

How will I tell Baba?

When I get up, my foot hits the cup. There goes the tea.

I make myself go next door to tell Khalaa Gaur. (She's not really my aunt but I call her Khalaa for respect.) She runs over bouncing her baby on her hip. She takes a look at Mor lying there, covers her mouth with a corner of her porani and starts wailing. I wish she'd stop. Mor always said wailing was haram.

Khalaa Gaur says, "Yes. She's dead." As if I was lying.

Then she sees her bratty son peeking at the door. She tells him to go get my father.

"I don't know where Agha went."

"Silly boy! Go find him. He's past the village, working on the new road!"

"But I don't know where that is! It's too far."

Khalaa Gaur takes a menacing step toward him and he runs off, but I doubt he'll tell Baba.

She looks around the darkened room. "Don't you have any rags or something? We must tie her up."

I find the cloth I use to wipe the dishes. It's clean. She hands me the baby and then tears three long strips. She passes the first strip under Mor's chin and ties it at the top of her head. It will keep Mor's jaw closed. With the second she ties Mor's feet together and with the third she ties her arms to her sides.

She wipes her hands on her dress. "There. At least she won't spread apart now."

I thought Khalaa would stay with me but she's got work to do.

"Don't worry, Jameela," she says. "We'll get some women together to bathe her for the burial."

When Baba arrives I can tell he doesn't know. For a moment I can't say anything. My throat is blocked. I just stare at him.

He's starting to look annoyed. I didn't even answer his greeting. He says it again.

I reply, "Wa alaikum assalam." It means on you be

11

peace, too, but I can't imagine ever having peace again.

Finally he says, "Where's your mother?"

I shake my head and look down at my lap. More tears come, dripping in a blur onto my useless hands.

He runs into the room. Then there's the strangest choking kind of noise I've ever heard. I rush to his side, practically holding him up so he doesn't fall.

Khalaa Gaur, true to her word, gets some women together and they bring buckets of water. They tell me to leave but I say I want to help. Khalaa Gaur frowns.

"This is a serious matter. You're very young. We can't have you getting all upset while we bathe her."

"I'll be good."

I've never seen a dead body being washed. I'm very good at staying out of the way, and yet being ready to help at the same time.

First we take a sheet and cover her. Then, working under the sheet, we remove my mother's clothes. I bundle them up and leave them in a corner. I'll wash them later. Maybe they'll fit me one day.

My mother looks younger with just the sheet lying over her. Muttering prayers, we gently clean her, make wudu for her, then wash her hair, the right side of her body, then the left.

She's gotten quite stiff. Her hands feel like they've been carved out of wood, a very soft wood, and her toes are splayed. I keep expecting her to open her eyes.

She looks peaceful and beautiful to me. She always said, "Jameela, if you can't be beautiful you should at least be good. People will appreciate that."

We don't have any camphor. I wish we did. It would leave such a nice scent.

When her body's clean, we're ready to wrap her. Despite the sheet that's covering her, I still catch glimpses of her body. It makes me feel so awkward. She was always so shy and modest. I can't remember ever seeing even her thigh. I try my best not to look.

Before the white cloth is wrapped over her face, I kiss her forehead. The women hesitate for just a moment, and then cover up the last of her.

Now we all need a bath.

Baba's outside with the men, sitting on the stony ground, looking as tired as I feel. While we were doing the ghusl they were digging her grave. May Allah make it spacious for her, Ameen.

Some of the women are wailing. They sound like the sirens of those foreign vehicles. It should bother me but it doesn't. It's funny how quickly you can get used to the sound.

Khalaa Gaur says, "I wish I could stay with you tonight, but my little one is miserable. You'll be okay."

I nod.

The last time someone died, our house was full of people, all coming with whatever food they could spare.

But then so many people were killed.

It doesn't look like that's going to happen this time. There have been too many funerals. People are weary. And with all the mines left behind in the fields, and the years of drought, there's little food.

13

The aunties leave for home. That's the signal for the men to come in and take my mother away, charpaee and all.

Let them be gentle. Don't let them bump the frame on the doorway. Don't let them jostle her as they make their way down the slope.

I watch until they turn a corner and I can't see them any more.

The ground is rocky. Pebbles poke at the soles of my bare feet.

The sun is beginning to set. The Afghan sky is flying banners of red and orange and yellow. Mor would have loved it. She adored color.

I get some more water. I'll have to clean up, too. Wash that sheet, wash her last clothes, her bedding. Just the thought of it makes me feel drained.

I bathe myself in much the same way we bathed my mother, and I put on my spare clothes as quickly as I can. I must hurry. Maghrib time passes so quickly.

I pray extra nafil for her and spend a long time in sujud, pressing my forehead to the rough fabric of my prayer mat, begging Allah to have mercy on her soul.

They must have finished her Janaza by now. They'll bury her before it gets too dark. I should make Baba some tea and see what there is to eat. The place is such a mess, and I'm so weary.

I'm just adding the tea leaves when he bursts through the door.

The sound scares me, and I drop some of the tea leaves in the fire. They go up in a puff of fragrant smoke.

14

Will he notice? Will he yell at me for wasting tea? I'm shaking so hard that the leaves bounce around in the little tin in my hand.

Put it down. Before you spill more. So I do.

He comes and stands right behind me, and I'm not sure why.

I hold my breath.

Then he drops his hand on my shoulder, and I flinch, but he isn't squeezing. He's not pressing hard. He's patting me. He's not angry. In fact he's telling me to step aside, that I must be tired, and he'll make the tea.

I move to the other side of the fire and he squats down in my place, adding more tea leaves, even though there's more than enough in the pot. He doesn't know how strong to make it.

There's no milk for the tea and only a little sugar, and there's half a piece of naan. It's a bit hard and stale but if he soaks it in the tea it will be fine.

When he looks up at me the shine of his eyes catches the glitter of the fire.

"Is this all the food in the house?" He points at the naan.

Is he angry? Does he know? Of course I should have saved all of it for him because he needs his strength, but I broke off a small chunk and ate it myself. Should I confess?

I huddle into my porani and nod. He could take it as a yes or maybe even an I don't know.

After a long pause, I lift my head to see what he's doing.

He's pouring the tea, and spilling a lot of it in the process. He hasn't the knack for it.

He hands me a cup and the whole piece of hard naan, but when I hesitate to take it he says, "Go on. You can have it, Jameela."

So I do. And such a surprise, my tea is sweet, too! He put the sugar in the pot for both of us.

He sips thoughtfully, staring at the fire. I wonder what he's thinking. Is he thinking of the last time we were a house in mourning?

When he sits up suddenly and takes a deep breath, I can't help flinching.

He's feeling at the pocket of his kurtha and he glances at me.

"You should get to bed. It's late now."

The night is cold. I hate to touch the water to make wudu but I must. I might as well get it over with. I wonder if Baba will pray with me. He prayed Janaza. He had to. There were all those people there, what would they think? But will he pray Isha tonight when there's no one but me to see him?

It doesn't look like it. He's gone back to staring at the fire.

It's hard to concentrate on my prayer with him in the room. It's so strange to see him here. At this time of night he's always out with his friends.

I finish quickly and then grab one of the quilts Mor made and wrap myself up. I'll wash the dishes in the morning. I lie with my back to the mud wall. That way it feels like I'm not so alone.

Baba drinks the last of his tea and gets up and stretches. His spine lets out a crack. He grabs another quilt, one Mor made from worn-out clothes, throws dirt on the fire and curls up in a corner.

He doesn't go into their room. I don't blame him.

Mor would have been sweeping the floor right now. Her silhouette would be passing by the fire, bobbing up and down in that funny squat-walk, holding the long broom bristles in her fist. I'd hear the calming *swish-swish* sound of the bristles brushing the floor. And she'd be laughing and telling me a story while she worked.

She was so full of stories. She told me once about how her father, my grandfather, used to mold clay pots on his wheel back when there was peace in Afghanistan. He said what made a pot strong was the firing. If the pot came out too soon, it would crack and be useless.

Mor said we're made of clay, too. Allah molded Adam from it, and we're the children of Adam. When things get bad, that's our firing. We have to be patient, trust in Allah that we will come out of it without cracking.

She's resting now, beyond sickness and pain and hunger. May Allah have mercy on her. Ameen.

I'm so tired but I can't sleep. This time yesterday she was alive. What if I had gone to her straight away this morning? What if I had stayed by her bed? What if I'd run to get the doctor in the next village? No. What if can drive you crazy. What if opens the door to shaitan.

Insha Allah, it will be better in the morning. If only I can sleep. If only I can get through tonight.

2

Something wakes me up, some noise in the blackness, like someone being sneaky. I huddle deeper into my quilt and I wait for the sound to come again.

A soft step. Then a bump and my father's voice muttering a curse. And then the unmistakable crinkle of aluminum foil and the click of a cigarette lighter. But he's not smoking a cigarette.

Mor made him promise. How many times did he promise? I can see his face now, lit up by the tiny flame. His eyes bulging. He doesn't see me watching. He doesn't care about anything but that little brown lump of opium smoldering on the foil.

There's a small tube pressed against his lips. Is it a piece from one of those foreigners' pens? He's using it to suck up the smoke.

Oh, the stink.

He holds his breath, keeping the smoke in like he doesn't want to let it go, but finally he must. Already the lines around his face have relaxed. His eyes are glazed. He's escaped into his own little world.

Nothing will make him angry now.

I can't watch him. It makes me sick. So I turn to face the wall and pull the quilt right up to my nose and tuck it tight around my head to keep out that smell.

Allah protect me. Allah have mercy on me. Watch over me and help my father.

The next thing I know I hear a banging at the door. What time is it? It must be late. There are cracks of daylight shining through the chinks in the door and shutters. More banging.

The hut is cold. I shiver as I push back the quilt and grab my porani. It's Khalaa Gaur with her baby perched on her hip.

It's warmer outside than it is in the hut, so I step out there to join her. The sun shining on my back feels good.

Khalaa Gaur peeks into the dark doorway and sniffs the air.

"What's that smell?"

Does it still smell? The stink should be gone by now.

She says, "I brought you something. It's not much."

Just seeing the naan in her hands makes me feel light-headed and weak with gratitude.

She glances past me at the darkness of the hut.

"Do you need help? I was going to start the fire for you and help clean up."

I invite her in, but then I hear a stirring from the pile in the corner. She stares at it.

"Your father's still here?! He's not digging gravel by the road?" She's frowning, thinking hard.

"I'll come back later," she says. "When he's gone."

She presses the naan into my hands, but instead of turning right to go back to her own hut, she goes left toward the huts of the other aunties. They'll be busy for quite some time, wagging their tongues about Baba.

Baba came here from Kabul when he married Mor. They've always hated him. They never trust outsiders, no matter how long you live among them.

There's water in the bucket. I pour some into the pot for tea. Baba groans when I strike the flint with the steel, and for a moment I freeze.

Don't wake up yet, Baba. The tea's not made.

He rolls over and settles back down. Good. A bit more time. But the spark has gone out. I have to strike the flint again, but this time Baba doesn't move.

Blowing on the tinder to get the fire to catch makes me feel dizzy. It's a mercy when the flames start licking the dry grass. Feed it small sticks, then bigger ones. Be patient or the fire will go out. And then sticks the size of my fingers, and now I can put on the pot for the tea. It will taste so good with the naan.

While that's boiling I'll gather the laundry. I hesitate in front of the door to the bedroom. I take a deep breath and push the door open.

It's dark. Nobody opened the shutters, but chinks of light are enough to let me see the pile of bedsheets and clothes that I dropped in the corner yesterday.

I grab them and back out of the room, shutting the door too quickly behind me. The sound of the door slamming wakes Baba, and instantly I freeze.

20

He rolls over, stretching his arms wide, a slight smile on his face like he hasn't got a care in the world. He sees me and stops, squinting up at me.

Is he wondering who I am? After a moment he smiles, but his voice is thick and blurry.

"Aah, Jameela. Where's your mother?"

Has he forgotten already?

The look on my face, the quiet of the hut, maybe that sobers him because suddenly he sits up and looks around. His shoulders slump and the smile is gone.

I pour him some tea. And I give him the naan. Will he take it all or will he give me some? Why didn't I break some off and hide it when I had the chance?

He doesn't ask where the naan came from. Maybe I should tell him.

I try to speak but my voice is hoarse. He looks up, waiting. I have to say something now. I clear my throat and try again.

"Khalaa Gaur…Khalaa Gaur, she came by earlier and gave us that naan."

"Oh." Then he looks down at the naan in his hands. "Did you have some?"

I huddle into my porani and shake my head.

"Why didn't you say something?!" He sounds almost angry, and instantly I'm tense and ready to duck. But he isn't lashing out. He breaks off a big chunk for me, bigger than what's left for himself, and hands it over.

I protest, saying I'll take the smaller piece.

"No. You have it," he says.

21

I protest again, but something in his face warns me, and finally I take the larger piece. He's tearing the naan, stuffing it into his mouth. His fingernails are so dirty. I try not to stare.

When he has finished, he combs his fingers through his hair and smooths out the wrinkles in his kurtha a bit. It doesn't help. He looks like he rolled off a cliff. And finally he leaves. For work, I hope.

With him gone a great weight has been lifted. It's good to have food in my stomach. I feel strong enough to tackle the washing.

I carry the clothes in a steel tub down to the river. Other girls are there already, slapping their laundry against the rocks to get the dirt out of them. They see me and stop talking, stop everything. And for a moment they just stare at me and I stare at them.

Then Nooriya, one of the kinder ones, jumps up and takes the tub from my hands.

"Jameela, you poor thing. Just rest over there. We'll wash these."

For a moment it feels nice. I feel like a queen resting beneath this tree while they work. But I can't hear what they're saying over the sound of the river and the slapping of the laundry.

And I feel itchy watching them do my work. In the end I join them and take back the task.

3

WHEN Mor was alive I would often avoid Baba. He had an unpredictable temper, and I didn't like the way he looked at my lip, like somehow it was my fault I was born this way. But with her gone he's been quite kind. On too many nights I still hear the crinkle of aluminum foil and the click of the lighter followed by the stink of burning opium, but then the next day he seems to be easier to live with.

Last night he smoked a lot, so I thought today he would be in an especially good mood.

But he wakes up scowling, rubbing the dirt from the corners of his bleary eyes with his filthy fingernails. His voice is fuzzy.

"It's this place. It's unlucky, that's what it is. We should leave here. Go to Kabul where I can get a proper job. There's all kinds of construction. That's where the real money is."

"Here, Baba. Have some tea. It will make you feel better."

"In Kabul we would have milk. There's all kinds of opportunity there. I'm sick of this!" And he waves his arm around his head to include the house, the village. And me?

23

"You're still tired, Baba. You'll feel better when you've had something to eat."

"Don't tell me what I am! I'll tell you!" He gets to his feet. The door slams behind him.

My face is hot. How could I have been so careless? So disrespectful. Maybe I'm tired, too.

Baba and his talk of luck. There's no such thing! Everything happens for a reason. We just can't always see it.

He hasn't been gone an hour when he comes running back. I'm spreading the laundry on tree branches to dry.

"Leave that and get packed. We're going."

Mor's quilt is wet and heavy. I struggle to heave it over a thicker branch.

He says, "What's wrong with you? Didn't you hear me? We're going. We're leaving this God-forsaken place!"

Asthaghfirullah! What a thing to say!

I've pulled my porani close to my mouth and realize I'm chewing on the end like I do when I'm nervous.

He's talking on, something about how nice it will be in Kabul, how he misses it, how the foreigners don't bomb that city. But I can barely hear him.

I push half of Mor's quilt over the branch. Almost there.

Baba grabs it from my hands and drops it back in the tub.

"Didn't you hear me? I said leave it! It's not even ours any more. I sold it. We can't carry all that stuff. Go inside and get packed. Listen to me or I'll…"

I'm chewing the corner of my porani again. He grabs my arm in a grip too tight and drags me into the house.

24

"Get your things now. I want to get there before night-fall."

But that's impossible. I've heard it's a three-day journey, even by donkey.

My spare clothes are still wet. And there are the pots and pans. I start to put them together in some kind of pile.

"Leave those, too. I sold them. Anything else?"

I hold out the matches and tinder. He grabs the tinder, just little tufts of dried grass, and tosses it to the ground.

"We won't need that. We might have real heat in the city."

It comes down to a small bundle of my wet clothes and my comb. He sold everything else. Even Mor's clothes. I won't be able to grow into them after all.

"Can I visit her grave? Say goodbye to her?"

Baba looks at me for a moment.

I'm waiting for him to decide.

Finally he says, "Just go. Be right back, though. Don't make me come to get you."

I run.

Down the stony hill and across the road, dust coats my feet and I slip once or twice, but it feels so good to be out. I pull my porani in so it still covers me. The leaves on the few remaining trees hang straight down and barely move.

The place is empty, the graves small humps of loose gravel and dirt. None of them have markers. There are two newer mounds but it isn't hard to figure out which is Mor's. The other one is the length of a child.

It's so quiet. No hint of a breeze.

Now that I'm here I don't know what to say. I wonder if she can hear me. Sense my footsteps above her.

Tearing off a corner of my porani, I wrap a large stone in the blue cloth and tie it tight, double knots that I pull with my teeth so they won't ever come loose. They would have laid her on her right side so she was facing Mecca. Her head would be on this side, so that's where I gently place my marker.

I wonder if she knows he's taking me away. I recite Surah Fatiha. It makes me feel better. Allah is with me even if she's gone.

It's like I can hear her. *Jameela, remember the man who asked the Prophet (peace be upon him) for advice. What did the Prophet (peace be upon him) tell him?*

"Don't become angry," I whisper. "Don't become angry. Don't become angry." He said it three times.

I'd better go before Baba comes looking for me.

"Assalaamu alaikum, Mor." Peace be upon you.

I turn toward home, but each step is a struggle. Something inside me is ripping.

I meet my father halfway. He was already coming to fetch me. When he sees me he just nods and turns around. I follow him closely even though it's hard to keep up.

He looks around at the mud house that was our home, checking the corners for anything forgotten. And then a horn sounds outside.

"He's here."

I pull my porani tight to my face. Who is this now? My head's in a whirl.

A battered truck is parked on the rocky area in front.

"Get in the back," Baba says. It's flat and open to the sky. Baba climbs into the cab, grabbing the agha's hand in a firm grip and smiling broadly.

Why is he so happy? Is this all just a big adventure for him?

I wish someone would come out and wave goodbye. Nooriya, Khalaa Gaur, one of the other neighbor aunties, even Khalaa Gaur's bratty son. No one's there to watch us pull away in a rattle of pebbles, me lurching left to right, gripping the side of the truck to keep from falling out.

The road barely exists. What isn't churned up by the tracks of military machines is pock-marked with bomb craters. These days the machines belong to the Americans, but before that they belonged to the Russians and in between those two invaders, we had the Taliban.

We've had nothing but misery for so long. All these foreigners fighting over us like dogs with a bone.

This agha cannot drive fast but as it is the wind plays like a devil with my porani. It's all I can do to keep covered. The sun beats down and I'm feeling hot and sticky in no time.

The mountains in the distance are a misty bluish color. During the Taliban years there was drought. The land has yet to recover. Even I can remember when the hills of Afghanistan were carpeted in green and everywhere there were flowers. Now it's just dull brown.

We pass through other villages. Villagers huddle together, sleeping on charpaees, tending to skinny goats. They glance at us respectfully as we drive by. What there is of traffic is all heading toward Kabul, mostly old men on donkeys loaded twice their height with straw and sticks.

Part of me is excited. How could I not be? It's my first ride in a vehicle. It's such a strange floating kind of sensation, this riding above the ground.

And I can't help feeling important. I've always made way for cars and trucks and now other people make way for us. Agha likes the horn. People rush out of our path as we pass, as if we're some kind of dignitaries.

But it's just a truck. Didn't I despise others when they acted like this? Mor always said Allah gives to whom He pleases. She said that having things doesn't make people better.

Am I forgetting her already? My eyes water and I wipe them dry.

No. I'll never forget her. No matter how far away he takes me.

We pass more villages that all look the same and we pass empty fields that can't be sown because of mines left over from the wars. We drive for so long that even my teeth feel rattled.

We stop once to refuel and eat. They pass me a piece of naan and the bottle of water. I try to wipe the top without them seeing. The agha pulls out a red can that was sitting in the back with me and pours the contents into the tank. Then we're on our way again.

As we get nearer to Kabul, the houses get closer and closer together, leaning up against each other like they're tired.

The air is yellow, and it tastes thick. How can they breathe? The exhaust of hundreds of cars clogging the roads makes me cough.

And everywhere there are people! I never dreamed there were so many!

They don't look friendly. They walk with their heads bent, scowls on their faces. And many of the women are bare-headed. There are ragged children everywhere.

My legs are cramped. I've been sitting for too long. I feel like getting out and walking, too. The roads are so clogged with traffic, I'm sure I'd make better speed.

We drive down a hundred lanes and alleys, barely squeezing through the houses in places. Finally we stop on a ragged broken pavement in front of a house that is definitely not made of mud.

While Baba's thanking the agha, I get my bundle together and my porani fixed up around me.

Will we be staying here? The men talk and talk and I wait and wait. It wouldn't be so bad if Mor were here. She'd nudge me under her porani, and I'd nudge her back, and from her eyes I would be able to tell she was smiling.

The agha puts a hand on Baba's shoulder and leads him in, calling to his wife to get some tea ready. He speaks Pushto with a thick Farsi accent.

Did they forget about me? Am I supposed to wait out here?

Finally Baba sticks his head out the doorway and waves at me to join them.

The house is cool and dim and smells like burnt onions.

29

My bare feet slap against the smooth cold floor. I've never been in such a grand home. They even have a beautiful wrought-iron gate that looks like it has a lock. That would keep them safe with so many bandits around.

We go down a narrow corridor to a room on our left that has a television in the corner and some corbacha on the floor. The corbacha are stuffed fat and so soft I could fall asleep right here.

A khalaa comes in, a porani barely covering her hair, nothing covering her face at all. The way my father gawks at her makes me burn with shame. When will he look away? Won't the agha be cross? And yet he doesn't seem to mind. Is he showing her off?

He gestures toward me and says, "Look who I've brought to help out? You'll just need to show her how you want things done."

Khalaa's face changes. She looks at me like she's wondering how strong I am. I sit a bit taller.

"Very well. Come here then."

I hate to leave those corbacha. I get to my feet and follow her into another room, less grand, with grease splattered on the walls.

There are some pots that need scrubbing. One of them contains the very charred remains of onions.

"Start with these," she says.

"Where's the ash?"

She wrinkles her nose.

"We don't use ash in the city! Here." And she hands me a plastic bucket filled with some kind of powder.

She sees my confusion and she hands me this curled-up metal stuff.

"This is soap. You pat the metal on it and scrub the pots. The water comes out of this tap here."

Water inside the house? No hauling buckets?

"I'll come back to check on you."

The sooner I start, the sooner I'll be done. I'm not sure how much of the soap to use. It looks like it costs a lot, so I'll just use a little so she won't get cross.

Soap is useless. I'd be done in a flash if I only had some proper fireplace ash.

I'm still struggling with the mess when a strange feeling of being watched comes over me.

A young girl is standing in the doorway. How long has she been there?

I smile at her.

"Assalaamu alaikum," I say. She doesn't smile back and she doesn't answer. What's wrong with her?

I turn back to the pots, but I can still feel her eyes on me. It feels so strange to be stared at by such a young child. Why doesn't she say anything?

I look quickly at her to catch her staring. She looks away. Then when I turn back to the pots, she's staring at me again. Does she know about my lip?

Khalaa comes in past the girl, touching her head gently. It reminds me of something Mor would do.

Khalaa inspects the pots and nods.

"All right, take the small one there and make some tea." Then she hands me a jug that's brim full of milk. So much!

31

My mouth waters at the sight of it.

I'm eager to show her how well I can work. Tea is my specialty. I can make it easily.

But where's the fireplace? I don't see it anywhere so I ask.

"Silly. We don't have a fireplace. We have gas." And she squats down by these blackened claw-like things and turns a knob.

I hear a hiss and there's a strange smell. She grabs a flint and some steel from the top of a little shelf, hits them together to make a spark and immediately there are tongues of blue flame licking the bottom of the black claw-like thing.

I see. She turns a knob to control how high the flame goes.

"All right, fill the pot with water and make the tea." So I do as she commands, taking a gulp of the water while I'm at it. Ew! City water stinks!

When she's gone I drink some of the milk. It tastes so good, washing away the taste of the city water. There's still plenty left for the tea.

My porani's in my way and the men are inside, so I tie it up around my head so it's away from those sneaky blue flames. Mor once told me about a lady from the village who was careless and her porani caught fire. Her neck was forever scarred by it.

When the tea is ready, I turn the gas down until the blue flames cough and sputter out.

Where's Khalaa? I don't have permission to enter the rest

of the house. Where's that girl then, the one who was staring at me? She's not here either.

I untie my porani so that it's covering me again and wait.

When Khalaa comes in, she looks ready to yell.

"What are you doing? It's getting cold! Pour it in the cups!"

I tell her I don't know where the cups are. She hasn't shown me. She makes a face like it's still my fault, grabs the cups and a tray and pushes them at me.

"Take them inside."

I adjust my porani again so it's covering my face, but it's hard. I hold the tray with one hand. I hope it doesn't fall. She might slap me.

Baba doesn't notice me. He's too busy laughing at the agha's joke.

I set the tray down and retreat to the kitchen. Khalaa hands me tea in a chipped cup. I sit down in a corner and drink it. The creamy buffalo milk almost hides the taste of the water.

Khalaa is standing at the side, her arm around that creepy girl, watching me and nodding.

I draw my porani around me so there's not much they can see. I'm sure Baba's going to get some money from my helping, and he'll be working for this agha. Maybe in a few months we can find our own place and set up a house.

The agha barges into the kitchen just then, glances at me and starts speaking in a strange language. I think it's Farsi. I recognize a few of the words.

Khalaa doesn't like it. In Pushto she says, "What are you talking about? I don't want you wasting all our hard-earned money!"

He glances at me, then replies in Pushto. "It's *him* paying."

I can't help stiffening. They're watching me so I try to relax. I wish I could take Baba aside, talk some sense into him. He's laughing and smiling, fingering the Afghani notes in the pocket of his kurtha — the money from all our things he sold — hurrying agha out of the house like he can't wait to spend it.

What could I say to him? Baba does what he wants. He and Mor were forever fighting over it. He wouldn't listen to her. Why would he listen to me?

Khalaa keeps me busy all evening. I change and wash the sheets of the beds upstairs, I sweep the stairs and wash the windows the best I can, one ear always listening for the rumble of the truck. I've prayed Isha and got ready for bed and I still haven't heard it.

"Here," says Khalaa, and she hands me a quilt. "You can sleep in this hallway. When the men arrive, let them in but first make sure it's them." And she shows me how to lock that fancy iron gate and bolt the door behind it.

I curl up on the floor. The house is full of strange creaking noises like someone is walking overhead. It was better when I was busy. I didn't have time to think of Mor lying in her grave so far away. I don't want to think of her body decaying but I can't help it.

All the bodies I've ever seen in different stages of decay

34

flash across my mind wearing Mor's face. Even our she-goat. The one who wandered into the minefield to graze. She wasn't ten feet from the path but we couldn't retrieve her. It was too dangerous. I can still see the maggots crawling at the corner of her eye, her blackened tongue and her belly swollen and ready to burst.

It's been a month since we buried Mor. Soon there will be nothing left of her that I can recognize.

I wish she hadn't died so soon. I wish she was here beside me. But she's gone. She said we're all headed that way.

The best thing I can do is be just like her. It won't be easy. She was so good. So patient, even when I made a mistake, never raising her hand to strike me, and when I was sick she never left my side except to get me some water to drink.

I wake to the sound of the truck pulling up. It's so loud! I unbolt the door and peek through the grill to make sure it's them.

But something is wrong. Agha opens the door and falls out of the cab. He's lying in a heap. And he's making noises, sobs, I think. Baba's not much better. He comes around to help him up and ends up falling on top of him.

Oh, Allah, please. Not him, too.

I run back to the stairway.

"Khalaa! Khalaa! Come quick. Something's wrong."

Khalaa comes rushing down the stairs, tossing her porani over her head.

"What's the matter? What happened?"

I'm struggling with the lock, but somehow the key won't turn. Khalaa pushes me out of the way and opens it easily.

My father smells so strange.

"They're ill! Shall I go for a doctor?"

Why is Khalaa so calm? Does she care that little for her husband? If only she'd tell me which way to run to get a doctor.

She flips the light switch, takes one look at them and sneers.

"They're not ill. They're drunk." Without a word she grabs Agha's arm and drags him inside.

Drunk?! But that's forbidden. Now I see that Agha wasn't sobbing. He was giggling.

My father has this stupid grin on his face, like he doesn't have a worry in the world. I guess I should bring him in out of the alleyway, although part of me is tempted to leave him lying there. He's so heavy and I'm so weary.

I guess I'm not as careful as I should be while dragging him. He lets out a moan when he bumps his head on the edge of the gate. I should feel bad about it, but I don't.

I've always been taught to respect my elders, especially my parents. With Mor it was easy.

4

THE PROBLEM with hard shiny floors that are not made of mud is that dust from the streets, from all the dung of donkeys and horses and animals in the alleyways — the same dust that clogs the air — ends up settling on those nice shiny floors, and they need to be swept and mopped every single day.

It takes me all morning. I always save Farzana's room for last. That's the name of the girl. She still hasn't spoken to me. Her tutor comes an hour before lunch time and I like to listen to her lessons.

The tutor is not an old woman. I'd say about Mor's age, but so very different. She has glasses and she's missing teeth. It's not hard to peek at the little slate that she's drawing on. *Alif, ba, ta.*

I could learn to read if I just had the chance. Mor always wished it for me but there was no school in the village, and she had grown up during the war when there was no such thing as school, so she couldn't teach me herself.

37

The tutor says, "Miss, I cannot help you if you do not complete your homework."

Farzana rolls her eyes. "My head hurts."

A whiny note creeps into the khalaa's voice.

"Miss, your mother pays good money for me to come to teach you. I have four children to feed. You'll get me in trouble if you don't learn anything."

Farzana yawns so wide that I can see the black spots on her upper back teeth.

The khalaa purses her lips and taps the slate with her pointy stick.

"Miss, please. What letter is this?"

Jeem. Say *jeem.* I think it so loud I'm sure Farzana can hear me. But she just frowns at the board.

"Ha?"

The khalaa sighs. "No, miss. *Ha* doesn't have the dot in the middle. Please concentrate."

Farzana shrugs. *"Kha?"*

The tutor sighs even louder.

"No, miss. *Kha* has the dot on top. This letter has it in the middle, right here, see?"

It takes five minutes to get Farzana to admit it's a *jeem.* And another five minutes to figure out that the letter makes the sound "ja."

I've finished the floors. I should go down and start making lunch and yet I dawdle. I'll just dust the furniture.

When her mother barges in, Farzana sits up, the tutor stands straight, and I wipe the furniture a bit faster.

Khalaa glances at me and frowns but doesn't say anything. She gestures for the tutor to come outside. The lady crosses the floor quickly and they have a whispered conversation in the hallway.

Farzana picks up her doll and starts changing its clothes.

I can't linger any longer so I go downstairs to make lunch.

I must admit the stove is a lot easier to use than our old fireplace. It didn't take me long to get the hang of it.

The nice thing about being the cook is that you never go hungry. I always make sure there's a little extra left for me.

The tutor eats in the kitchen with me. I've got my porani all wrapped up around me, making a kind of tent. She avoids looking my way. If I lived with her, I could learn so many different things.

I shouldn't be thinking like this. She has four children already. What does she need with another mouth to feed? I should be grateful for what I have, not longing for things that are out of reach.

Khalaa comes in after I've washed the pots and picks up one of them to see if there's any dirt left inside. She squints and looks close. She rubs at a mark, but I know I did a good job. I'm very careful, and I try to please her.

She picks up another and does the same.

I'm glad I have my face covered. She can't see me smile. She gets angry when I smile.

In the end she can't find anything wrong so she has to just nod and go away.

She's been talking Farsi a lot more. She thinks that way I can't understand, but it's not that hard to pick up what they're saying. Especially since she's not very good at speaking it and she mixes in a lot of Pushto words. Plus she has this habit of looking at what she's talking about. I'm learning a lot, but I make sure I keep my face neutral. I don't want her to stop teaching me.

It's Jumaa so the tutor's not coming today. Farzana's skipping around the kitchen, knocking over the pile of dishes I still need to rinse. I'm in the middle of scrubbing the tea pot when Khalaa calls me away.

"Jameela, I'm going to have a dinner party tomorrow and you're going to need to wear some nicer clothes. Here are some of my old things. I want you to get cleaned up and wear them tomorrow. And get rid of that shawl on your head. It's getting ragged. This is the city. Such country fashions don't go here."

My porani's only ragged because I can't stop chewing on the corner. I'm chewing on it right now.

"You want to see the dress I'll be wearing?" She doesn't wait for my reply but goes to her wardrobe and pulls out a very short, very small dress. It would fit Farzana properly but it will only go to Khalaa's knees!

"I kept it from the days before the war," she says. "Back then we got fashions from Paris! My aunt was expert at copying them. And I'll do my hair up in a bun."

Why is she telling me all this? Why would she think I want to know?

I get a creepy feeling down my back and turn around. Farzana's standing by the door. She looks at me and struts past.

"Oh, that's beautiful! What will I wear?"

The two of them are so excited, tossing frocks on the bed, holding them up against themselves to see which ones suit them best. And yet it all feels so strange. They're talking so loud. They keep glancing at me out of the corners of their eyes.

Do they think I'm that stupid? After a few more moments of the show, I realize that they do. They really do think I'm just a stupid villager.

I clear my throat and say respectfully, "Khalaa, the tea things are getting dried out, and I still haven't rinsed the soap off them. May I go?"

Khalaa frowns and then nods.

"Don't forget what I said about that shawl of yours."

I'm chewing on the end even as I leave and make myself stop. If she thinks I'm getting rid of this porani, she's mistaken. Mor gave it to me, and no one can take it away.

I was worrying about all the cooking for this grand dinner party, but I needn't have. Khalaa isn't trusting me to do it. I guess I should be insulted but I'm only relieved. That would have been a lot of work! But I do have to turn the house upside down. Take all those fancy cushions outside and beat the dust out of them.

I spend over an hour whacking at those cushions until not a puff of dust rises even when I hit them my hardest.

A few hours before the party, men arrive with big pots and firewood. They build a stove right in the dirt of the alleyway. I've never seen men cook in such a big pot and use a shovel to stir it.

41

I'm wearing the new clothes Khalaa gave me and my old blue porani. Khalaa's wearing pointy high-heeled shoes. They make a lot of noise on the floor as she comes up behind me, *click, clack, click, clack.*

I don't turn around.

She taps me on the shoulder.

"I thought I told you to get rid of that old thing."

"I can't. I'm wearing the new clothes you gave me." And I lift the corners of my porani. "See?"

She frowns. "I don't like being disobeyed. Take it off. Now."

I take a deep breath. If she wants to walk around half-naked I don't care, but why should I?

"Khalaa, I need to wear it. It is our custom. Please understand."

I wait. She's chewing her lip. Finally she nods.

"Okay, then. But change it for tonight. I'll get you a better one."

"Oh, may Allah bless you," I say, and I mean it. She really isn't so bad.

When the guests arrive I can better understand why she didn't want me wearing it. The men are wearing western clothes. Pants and jackets and ties. The women have on short tight dresses like the one Khalaa showed me.

How they stare at me, not even covering their mouths to hide their giggles. When I serve a tray of sugar-covered almonds, one of the ladies laughs and says in Farsi, "Just looking at her makes me hot!"

And here comes that smell again. The one that covered my father that first night he came home drunk.

42

As the night wears on it gets worse and worse. Men dancing with women, touching them, pawing them, rubbing against them, and the women just toss back their heads and laugh. What's wrong with this agha? He sees his wife in the arms of every man and he doesn't even care?

Just when I think it can't get any more shameful, my father arrives and joins them. Wiggling like he's got a scorpion trapped in his pants. He looks like a fool. I've seen some of those foreigners' movies that Khalaa watches, at least parts of them. And even I can tell he's not copying them right.

As the night passes and the drinks flow, the men and women get loud and clumsy and I'm stuck on the side waiting for Khalaa's orders. They eat and drink and drink some more. And when they go back to eat again, the rice is falling out of their mouths because they forget to shut them while they chew. So much of it lands on Khalaa's nice red carpet, grinding itself in. It will be terrible cleaning it tomorrow.

The worst of it all is seeing my father. I didn't realize he was this bad. Mor used to say things sometimes when he came home late from work or after being out with his friends, but I never knew until now what she meant. I wish he wouldn't dance with Khalaa. He seems to go to her the most.

Long into the night I'm stuck there serving them. Farzana's supposed to be sleeping but I see her many times peeking from the staircase.

Finally, toward Fajr time, they start to leave.

Agha is unconscious in a corner, his mouth hanging open. Khalaa shakily sees her last guest off and turns around, tottering on her high heels like she's going to fall off them. I rush to her side and prop her up.

It's difficult getting her up the stairs in those heels. When we get to her room she collapses on the bed face first. I remove her shoes so she'll be more comfortable and pull the blanket across her back. She's still got her makeup on. Her pillowcases will be covered in it, and who will have to get those stains out but me?

I turn her over and get some wet tissues from the bathroom. The makeup comes off in heavy smears of red and blue and black. The tissue looks bruised by the end of it.

Without the makeup, Khalaa looks younger. I look out the window at the eastern sky. It's alight with dawn. The whole city sleeps, even though it's Fajr time.

I'd better hurry. I make my wudu and pray downstairs in the living room on top of my old blue porani. When I pick it up off the carpet, it has bits of crushed rice clinging to it.

Agha is passed out on the cushions. My father is not far from him, his legs straddled open, the fabric of his tight pants straining at the crotch.

I grab my comforter from the closet and lie down in the hallway, not far from those two. It will be strange sleeping with my porani on but I've done it before. My muscles ache with fatigue. Lying down feels so good.

I'm so tired I can't sleep. And tears arrive like unwelcome guests in the corners of my eyes.

There is no reason for me to cry. I've done nothing

44

wrong. So then why are my eyes dripping? Why is my chest bursting with sobs?

Telling myself to stop only makes the tears come faster. I feel like disaster lies just around the corner, and there's nothing I can do to stop it.

I turn my back to this wicked house and face the wall, snuggling into my little corner, stuffing the corner of my blue porani in my mouth.

Don't become angry. Don't become angry. Don't become angry.

Gradually my fists unclench. In the growing light I can see the grooves that my fingernails have pressed into the palms of my hands.

5

I know I'm dreaming. And in my dream I can see my father get up, peek at Agha lying on the cushions snoring, and creep like a thief up the stairs. And then I see scenes from the party—leering faces, twisting in and out of shape.

I want to wake up, I want to scream, I want to shout.

Am I? There's noise coming out of my mouth but I don't feel myself making it.

It isn't me. It's coming from upstairs. I wrap myself up and run up those stairs two at a time. Agha is there ahead of me, screaming at my father to get out, slapping his wife's head. And Farzana, darting in between, making the most noise of all.

I grab my blue porani but don't have time to get my comb. I have to leave it behind as we're literally shoved onto the street.

What did Baba do? No. I don't want to know. He's not looking at me. He's looking straight ahead, just marching down the alleyway as if he's got a plan, walking so quickly it's hard to keep up.

The street's getting crowded. He doesn't even look behind to see if I'm there.

"Baba! Wait!"

He hears and turns around, as if he's being generous and understanding and I'm being inconsiderate to keep him waiting.

He walks a bit more slowly now. And finally he turns to me and says, "Don't worry. I've got something better for us. It was time to move on anyway."

But I can't help worrying.

We go in and out through alleyways until finally we get to a small house, partially ruined, either by bombs or by neglect, I can't really tell.

A young man on crutches opens the door. He leans on one side and gestures for us to come in, as if he's expecting us.

I don't trust the look of him. It's got nothing to do with the crutches. He notices when I pull my porani in a bit tighter, and he grins in a disgusting way.

I step close to Baba and tug on his sleeve. He waves me off. I tug again.

"Stop it!" he hisses.

A lady comes in. She's wearing tight Punjabi clothes, and her porani isn't even on her head at all, and barely covering her chest. She's older, too, with wrinkles.

Baba greets her like they're old friends.

"I'm ready to make the arrangements. We'll keep it simple. Just the mullaa and a few witnesses."

The lady smiles so wide.

47

"Yes. And a few relations." She gestures to the man on the crutches. "Masood, dear, go to the market and pick up some meat. We'll have a feast tonight."

Mullaa? Feast? What?! Is Baba going to marry her? Just like that?

Baba finally seems to remember me.

"Jameela, this will be your new mother."

The lady smiles with her mouth but not with her eyes.

"Welcome to your new home."

I guess it could be worse. At least we'll have part of a roof over our heads.

My mother-to-be takes us on a tour of the house, at least the half that's standing. A high wall surrounds a large courtyard. The buildings on the right are rubble. On the other side is what's left of the house: three rooms and a kitchen. Once upon a time it might have been as grand as the place we just left.

The lady has a wardrobe full of her dead husband's clothes. They're from another time and too big on Baba, but he finds a nice suit to wear and they even find some new clothes for me.

How can this be a bad thing? At least Baba won't be looking at another man's wife. Maybe she'll be a nice mother. In any case, we'll have a roof over our heads, we'll be family. You can't kick out family no matter what they do. Before I was working hard for Khalaa. Now I'll be working hard for her. I'll try to be nice to her. I'll do my best, even though she could never take the place of Mor.

I spend all afternoon in the kitchen cutting vegetables

and stirring pots of food. She's much harder to please than Khalaa. Several times I cut the onions too thick and the carrots too thin. I'll have to try harder. At least I'm away from Masood's bold stare.

The mullaa arrives. He's a fat man wearing a white kurtha and a chitral hat. I thought my new stepmother would be the type to invite a lot of people, but in the end only her sister's family comes. Where are the others?

The sister looks just like her, but more pinched. Her nose is pointier and she has a sour expression. Her husband smiles a lot but doesn't say much. He has very few teeth and a moustache. Three of their kids are chasing each other around the coffee table, tripping on wrinkles in the red and black carpet.

It's while I'm frying almonds, raisins and sliced carrots in butter that I hear my stepmother and her sister whispering in the hallway just outside the kitchen.

Her sister says, "What are you thinking? You can do better than this. They look like beggars!"

"You don't know what it's like to lose a man. Look at my son, look at my house. It will be all right. You'll see."

"But that girl! She's already looking down her nose at you. She'll be cozying up to Masood before you know it."

"Never!"

"Sister, this is crazy."

"Sssh. They'll hear. Never mind. I've got plans."

Then they hustle into the big room to get ready for the nikah.

Do I really look down my nose at them? And if I do, don't they do the same to me?

Still, Mor wouldn't like it. She'd want me to do my best to get along with them.

My father's calling me to join them. I clutch the corner of my porani to my face. I wish I was wearing my old blue one, even if it is ragged.

I join the women. The men are around the corner in the other part of the room. The mullaa starts reading his marriage khutba. It's in Arabic so I don't understand a word. I wish I did. It's the language of the Quran. I would love to know what it really says.

We get to the part where Masood, acting as walee for his mother, offers her hand in marriage to my father. A crazy part of me wants to scream "No!" and drag my father out of here.

I shove the corner of my porani into my mouth to keep silent. Quietly my father accepts the offer, three times. The witnesses lend their blessing. My father presents the mehr to the woman. It is all the money he has left from selling our things. Then it's done.

I smile as big as I can, trying to look as happy as possible. My stepmother feels stiff when she hugs me. Maybe she's just not a hugging type of person. It feels so strange and then it occurs to me that it's been a long time since anyone has hugged me or even touched me. And then I think back to when was the last time. It was Mor, the night before she died.

I fetch the platter of basmati rice covered in the

almonds, strips of carrots and raisins that I just fried. There's chicken and koftas, little balls of spicy meat in a rich red sauce. They took a long time to make. And we have some kebabs as well, sprinkled with sliced onions and coriander leaves.

It's the second night in a row that we've had rich food, but tonight I actually feel like eating.

We all eat from one platter. Mor loved almonds, but she would have thought serving them like this was strange. We don't put them in rice. Maybe this is what they do in Kabul. I pick out the almonds and put them to the side of my food. I'll save them for later.

My new aunt and stepmother are eating quickly, cramming the food into their mouths and the mouths of the children. There's only one kofta left. Where did it all go?

I reach for it but Khalaa snatches it first. Then she gives me a look and smiles. She passes it to her daughter.

That's okay. I'll have a kebab. There are two of those left.

I reach for one but my new stepmother has picked them up. Both of them at once.

When she sees me pull my hand back, she says, "Oh, did you want one?"

"It's okay," I say, but secretly I hope she'll give me one. She doesn't.

A look passes between her and her sister and finally it hits me. I'm so dumb. They did it on purpose.

The chicken's all gone, too. Oh well. At least my belly's filled with rice. And I have the almonds.

They're shiny with butter and taste so good.

The men take out a large drum and start playing. The women get up to dance. I thought these people were different. I thought they were more traditional. Women dancing in front of men! But I guess we're all family now.

I pull my porani in closer to myself and huddle into my corner. I know I'm looking down my nose at them but I can't help it.

6

WHAT AM I supposed to call her? Not Mor. Never Mor.

If I'm careful, I probably won't have to call her any-thing.

The guests have all gone and a strange silence has descended. Those kids were messy. There's spilled rice and chicken bones under the sofa.

"Jameela, gather up the dishes…dear, and start cleaning them."

I hardly slept last night and I've been helping them cook all day. The muscles in my arms and legs complain.

"Couldn't I do them in the morning?"

Baba gives me a look. "Listen to your mother."

I nod and get to my feet. It's going to be a long night.

This lady doesn't have fancy powdered soap in a bucket. I use fireplace ash to wash the dishes. When I come out to look for more things to wash I realize that she and my father have gone into their room and left me alone with Masood.

"Little sister, now that we're family, you don't need to cover up in front of me like that."

I frown. I'm not sure what the ruling is about such things. But I'm not taking the chance.

There's a cup sitting on a low table beside him. I ask him to pass it to me.

He makes a face. "I can't reach."

It's right beside him.

I just leave it and take the rest of the stuff into the kitchen.

By the time I've finished all the washing, it's late and I'm exhausted. Masood has gone to bed. It's been a long day. I pray Isha. I don't know where I'm supposed to sleep so I curl up in a corner of the main room. It's quite comfortable with this carpet beneath me.

Better than the floor at that first place.

I hear giggling. It must be her.

I should fall asleep instantly. I'm so tired and yet I lie here staring into the darkness.

Then I see a shadow move in the corner of the room and I sit up. What is it? A rat? I reach into the pocket of my dress for the matches I keep there. Where's that little clay oil lamp? It was on the table beside where Masood was sitting.

I'm making a lot of noise, and the black shadow runs along the far wall. By the time I have light, it's gone beneath the crack of the door.

I carry the lamp by its little handle and step out into the courtyard. The stars are shining brightly. Kabul is quiet and deeply cold. I pull my porani close. The pile of rubble across the courtyard is a huge mound. I see a sil-

54

houette outlined against the stars. It's too big for a rat so I raise the lamp higher. Two eyes glow green in a jet black face.

A cat. Suddenly I feel a bit safer.

It bends its head, sniffing the rubble. Its fur is snarled and one of its ears is torn. A battle-scarred warrior. I slip back into the room and lie still, feeling a bit better.

Maybe things will be all right. Didn't Khalaa at the other place seem like she would be terrible? And wasn't I able to win her over with hard work? Why should it be so different with my new stepmother? She has more reason to like me. If I can't be beautiful at least I should be good. I'll work hard and I'll do it without complaining.

Before I know it my eyes have opened from a restful sleep. The darkness has turned into a dim grayness. Dawn is on its way.

I have to break a thin film of ice off the surface of the water in the jar to make wudu. I use as little water as possible but even then I'm shivering. After Fajr, I start the fire and sweep out the kitchen area with the broom. I wonder how my stepmother likes her tea.

There's a little buffalo milk but I don't see any sugar. There's also a bit of food left over from the wedding feast. It might be too soon to heat it. Who knows when they'll wake up?

I hear some rocks falling outside and run to see what it is. It's that black cat again. It's got the body of a huge rat in its mouth. It ignores me, climbing the rubble to get away.

When I turn to go back inside, Masood is standing in the doorway.

How long has he been standing there? My porani is open, my face is showing. Quickly I cover myself up but it's too late. He's already had a good look.

"No wonder you hide yourself."

"That's not why I cover! I would cover myself even if I was the most beautiful girl in the world. Especially if I was beautiful!"

He shushes me with his hand.

"I know, I know. I'm just teasing. What's wrong with your lip?"

I shrug. "I was born this way."

He's standing right in the middle of the doorway. I'd have to go too close to squeeze past. I guess he sees me hesitate, and then, ever so slowly, he moves himself over with his crutches, as if he's being polite.

I'd like to kick that crutch out from beneath him. See him fall flat on his face.

With a little hop step, he follows me into the kitchen.

"Did you make me some tea?"

I did, but now I wish I hadn't. I point at the pot.

He looks at me for a moment like he expects me to pour it for him, but I won't.

"Help yourself."

He puts both of his crutches together, leans heavily on the crossbar in the middle of them and lowers himself down to the floor. He lays them on the side and then picks up the pot by its handle.

Then he realizes that the cup is sitting on a shelf above him.

By this time I feel kind of sorry for him so I reach over to get the cup, but he says, "No! I'll do it myself."

Painfully he pulls himself up the same way he lowered himself down, grabs the cup in his teeth and lowers himself back down again. His leg looks so strange where it's missing below the knee. He pours himself the tea and sits back, cupping it in his hands like he's cold.

I grab another cup, squat down and pour myself some tea, too.

It's so easy for me. Subhanallah. The things I take for granted.

"What happened to your leg?"

"Landmine."

"How old were you?"

He pauses. "You ask a lot of questions."

"We're family now, I guess."

"I was ten, playing soccer in a field. I didn't know there were mines."

"That's a stupid way to get hurt. I thought you at least lost it fighting the Russians."

He looks at me sharply.

"I'm not that old."

"What happened to your father?"

He shrugs. "The Americans killed him. Three years ago. He died in prison."

His silence makes me squirm. It makes me wish I hadn't asked. His lips are twitching or something. Is he trying not to cry?

57

In a hoarse voice he says, "What about you? Where's your mother?"

At the thought of her, tears prick my eyes. There's no nice way to put it so I just blurt it out.

"She got sick and died."

He nods, like he's not surprised at all.

"Where's the rest of your family?" he says.

"Gone."

"What do you mean? Did they go somewhere?"

"They're dead."

"All of them?"

I nod and hope he doesn't ask any more questions.

"What happened? How could they all be gone?"

I stare at him for a moment. I've never talked about it to anyone. And now my throat is tight. I might cry. Will he make fun of me? What can I do if he does?

It doesn't matter so I tell him.

"My father's family is originally from Kabul. Most of them died and the others left for India. We don't know where they are now. My mother's family is mostly dead, too. One of my mother's cousins was getting married. They were so happy!"

"And your family, they were shooting in the air to celebrate." It isn't a question. He knows.

"They were bombed."

"How come you didn't die?"

"We didn't go. My father was fighting with one of my aghas."

Masood says, "One of my aghas was blown up. He looked like a pile of bread crumbs."

I nod. There usually isn't a lot left of them.

I say, "My father recognized my agha, the one he was fighting with, by a piece of his jaw. The villagers helped us gather them up. We didn't bother trying to separate the parts into who was who. We just buried what we could find in one box. I'll never forget the smell."

I don't tell Masood that my father hasn't been the same since. Even if he is family he doesn't have to know that.

Quietly Masood says, "That was a very big test. The stronger you are, the harder Allah will test you."

I pull my porani a bit closer even though I'm not feeling cold. Mor said the prophets were always tested the worst. And then the believers. She said there's always one moment when you either pass or fail.

"Sometimes your test is a huge thing, and sometimes it's little," I say.

Masood pours more tea into his cup.

"Do you think your leg was your test?" I say.

He takes a sip and frowns.

"I don't know. I hope there's not too much more coming."

"Me, too."

He picks up his crutches. He's ready to get up. But before he goes, one thing is still bothering me. Any way I say it, it will sound rude. But I've got to ask.

"How did all this happen?"

"What?"

I point in the direction of his mother's bedroom.

"You know. This."

"My mother." He pauses and grimaces like he tastes something bad. "She wanted it. And well, I met your father and he seemed okay. He was always laughing and joking at the job site. Anyway, our boss liked him and your father came over for the past few weeks. And then yesterday, all of a sudden, he made up his mind."

I can just picture that last scene at the other place and why he made up his mind. My face gets hot. I look up to see Masood watching me.

He's about to say something when we hear some heavy footsteps approaching. His eyes flick back to the doorway and he whispers, "If you want to get along with my mother, learn to stay out of her way."

Before I can ask him what he means, the door flies open and she appears holding the cup I left sitting on that low table.

"What are you two whispering about in here?"

Masood says, "Nothing!"

My stepmother looks at me carefully. I say nothing. I don't even squirm under the force of her glare. I have not done anything to be ashamed of. I won't let her make me feel guilty.

Finally she says, "What happened to washing this? What other dirty dishes can I find lying around this place?"

Masood touches his mother's arm. "Mor. Gentle."

I jump to my feet. "I'm so sorry. I'll wash it right now. I made some tea... Would you like some?"

Her face softens a bit and she glances at the cups we were using.

"Make it hot. And warm me some of the food from last night. I'm starving."

In no time I have the rice sizzling in a pan and the tea bubbling. There's no meat left, but there are some almonds. My stomach rumbles and I realize that I'm hungry, too, so I snatch a few of the nuts.

She'll never miss them.

She sits down right there in the kitchen, grabbing a folded plastic tablecloth as a mini dusterkhan and starts eating. Pushing the plate toward Masood, she gestures to him to join her, then she glances at me.

"Would you like some?"

Masood looks away, embarrassed.

She actually asked me. I can't say yes. It would be too rude, so I shake my head and pull my porani around me.

She doesn't insist. When there's a third of the rice left she tells Masood to cover it and leave it for my father.

7

I CAN feel my neck muscles bulging, straining with the weight of these bricks. I can't hold them any longer.

"Where should I put them?"

"Just wait a minute while your father gets that side ready," my stepmother says.

I can't, and they drop while I jump out of the way so they don't crush my toes. They bounce off the dirt of the court-yard. Eight bricks out of the hundreds or thousands that are still piled up. My stepmother has decided we're going to save what we can of them. Baba's going to get some cement and we'll rebuild the ruined walls.

Lucky Masood. He only has to carry two at a time.

I wish I had shoes. I'm so scared I'll lose a toe.

My stepmother has her hands on her hips.

"Pick those up right now. And be careful next time! I don't want any of them cracking!"

"Yes, *Mother.*"

At the end of the day my fingers are scratched white and bleeding in places, and I'm sore all over.

Making supper hardly even seems like work in comparison. She sent Baba to the market this morning and he brought back some eggplant, potatoes and yogurt. I'm making banjaan. We'll have it with naan.

I slice the eggplant and potatoes extra thin so that she won't think they're too thick. Same with the onions. I take my time, adding ground-up garlic, salting the yogurt so that when it's drizzled on top it will bring out the best of the flavor. It takes me longer than usual.

Baba and Masood are still out there moving the bricks around. It's almost dark by the time I call them in.

As Baba passes me, I say, "It's Maghrib time."

"Then go pray," he says. "Take Masood with you."

Baba's not praying again? Neither is she, but at least she might have an excuse if she's mensing.

By the time Masood and I have finished praying, my father and his wife are using toothpicks to get the eggplant seeds out from between their teeth. There's not much food left. My stepmother grabs a piece of eggplant and holds it up to the light.

"What is this? Were you making paper? And the potatoes and onions, too? They practically disappeared in the sauce!"

Baba laughs and takes the flimsy piece of eggplant from her hands.

"If you needed more eggplant, you should have told me. I could have bought more." Then he pops it in his mouth.

Masood sends me a sympathetic look but doesn't say anything. What can he say?

We sit down with the remaining food and eat slowly. He's very considerate. There isn't much but he keeps pushing food over to my side. I'm tempted to just take it but I don't like being less polite, so I quietly push some of the food back.

He smacks his lips.

"Mmm. Wonderful, little sister!"

I can't stop a big silly grin on my face. It's ridiculous how much his bit of praise means to me. The naan is all gone so at the end we use our fingers and lick the platter clean.

The problem with making banjaan is that it takes so many pots. And now I have to wash them.

I haul myself to my feet and collect the dishes. She and Baba are still drinking from their cups. I'd like to take those cups with me now or I might forget and she'll yell at me again. I figure the less chance I give her to yell the sooner she'll start liking me. So I stand in front of them and wait.

She's in the middle of saying something to my father, laughing. It's a big joke, and out of the corner of her eyes she glances at me, but continues talking. My feet hurt, so I shift from side to side while I'm waiting. Baba doesn't notice me standing here at all. The dishes are getting heavy, so I shift them so I have a better grip. I wouldn't want them to fall.

I hope she'll take a breath soon, so I can ask her if she's finished with her cup.

Suddenly she turns to me and says, "What is your problem? Can't you wait until I've finished talking? Why are you always in such a hurry?"

64

I look at Baba, but he just looks away.

She's richer than we are. We need her.

She goes on, "Didn't you ever learn any manners? It's not polite to listen to people's conversations. If you expect to be welcome in this house you'd better learn that quickly. I can't stand nosy children."

"But I was just waiting to ask you for your cup. I was going to wash it."

She frowns.

"Well! Why didn't you say so?"

She drinks up the last bit in her cup and then reaches over and hands me Baba's, too.

When I turn to go into the kitchen, she adds, "And make sure you get those things properly clean. I don't want to see any food left behind." Then she turns back to Baba.

Baba says, "About your sister."

"As I was saying, when my sister got married they made an extension to their house and they rented it out. I'm thinking that we could rebuild the other side and do the same."

And they start talking about how much money that will bring in.

Before I leave the room I glance back at Baba. He's looking my way but I'm sure he doesn't see me. He's got a strange grin on his face and his eyes are gleaming.

Must be all that talk of money.

As I step into the kitchen the power goes out. It might be out for hours. It reminds me of life in the village. But it will be hard to make sure the dishes get properly clean.

I fetch the little lamp and wash the dishes by its weak light. After I've scrubbed them, I run my hand along them to feel if there's any crusted-on food left behind.

Masood comes in just then. I don't bother pulling my porani across my face. In this light he can't see much anyway. I hate to admit it, but it's almost nice to have him here.

"Masood, did you hear what they're planning to do?"

He nods. "This idea might actually work. There are lots of people coming to Kabul and they need homes."

"Maybe with all that money they'll be able to buy you a leg. I've seen them in the marketplace. I'm sure you could find one to fit you. You've probably finished growing, so it would be a good time to get one."

A look comes across his face that makes me pause in my scrubbing. It must be hard for him.

I can feel it as soon as she enters the doorway. A kind of chill sweeps across the room. Even Masood stiffens like he's bracing himself.

She says, "Are you finished with those pots yet?"

I try to sound cheerful. "All done!"

She looks surprised, like for a moment she can't think of what to say.

"Okay, then, come in here and sweep this floor. There's crumbs all over it."

I carry the lamp into the other room. It's so dark I can't see the dirt.

"Could I wait till the power comes back on?"

She bends her neck toward me, watching me suspiciously.

66

I keep my face straight. I have such a feeling, one wrong move and she'll pounce.

Finally she says, "Okay. When the power goes on you get it done right away. Don't make me come and find you. I don't want any dirt in any of the corners. I'm sure there are rats about. And make sure you get under the sofa, you hear me?"

I nod.

"Well, I guess you have some time to do what you want till then."

I go out into the courtyard. I wonder if that cat is there.

It's a cold clear night and the stars are so bright, they feel close, almost close enough to touch. There's a slight breeze blowing in from the east. It makes me shiver and pull my porani in.

I hunch down against the wall of the house. It's a little warmer here.

I pick up a stick, and in the dirt at my feet I scratch out a *jeem*. And then a *ha*, without the dot, and then a *kha* with the dot on top.

Jeem, for Jameela. I wish I knew the other letters.

The door opens suddenly and I quickly rub out the letters I've been drawing.

It's Masood.

"What are you doing?"

"Nothing. Just practicing letters. Do you know how to read?"

He nods. "Do you want me to show you?"

He picks up my stick and writes out the alphabet. I get to my feet.

· "No, wait. Write it over here, where it won't get messed up and I can look at it in the day."

He shrugs. "Okay."

With each letter he says its name and I repeat it. It feels like a secret that is finally being revealed to me.

"How do you write my name?"

It's all one long series of strokes. It's beautiful. And I was right. It does start with a *jeem*. I can see it there, right at the beginning, with that little curly part and the dot under-neath.

I pick up the stick to copy it when I hear a footstep behind me.

It's her.

"What's going on here?"

I jump to my feet and spin around. Masood looks incredibly guilty. My stepmother tries to see behind us but we both block her view.

She shoves me to the side and I land on the heap of bricks. Bending over, she peers at the marks in the dirt.

"What is this? Masood, why are you wasting her time?" Then she turns to me. "Don't you know the power's back on? Get in there and sweep that floor."

"Yes, *Mother*."

I hope she doesn't erase those marks. I wish it so hard. I would do anything she wants, if she just doesn't erase those marks.

Then I hear her yelling at Masood.

"Stop filling her head with useless ideas! They won't make her a better worker!"

68

Masood mumbles something I can't make out.

"What did you say?" she hisses.

"What does it have to do with you if I teach her?" he says.

And I hear a slap, flat on the top of his head. He gets to his feet and rushes to his room.

She's still yelling after him and then I can hear her rubbing her feet on the ground.

The sound of rubber sandals erasing the letters in the dirt is unmistakable.

8

IT'S NOT eavesdropping if your father and stepmother are yelling so loudly in the next room that you can't help but hear.

She says, "I'm telling you I've tried my hardest to be patient, but there's no getting along with her! And now she's turned my own son against me! With all I've done for him. I never thought I'd see the day when he would raise his voice to me, and for her!"

My father murmurs something that I can't hear.

"What's talking going to do? She doesn't listen. She can't even do simple little things right. I know what she's thinking when she looks at me, and I can't stand it any more."

I hear the clink of glass on glass. He's taking another drink. I can almost picture him lifting that disgusting smelly stuff to his lips. He says something again.

And she says, "He'll be getting married one day. His wife will..." The rest is garbled.

I pick up the pot that I am supposed to be scrubbing

70

and attack it with all the energy I have left. When I've finished it's cleaner than I've ever seen it before.

Maybe she's right. Maybe I haven't been putting in enough effort. It's not like when I did things for Mor.

Mor. Why did she have to die? If she were here I wouldn't be in this situation.

Am I questioning Allah's will? Like Baba? Asthaghfirullah! She would be so mad at me for thinking like this.

Sometimes I wish I could just lie down and not wake up. Die while I'm still good, before I have a chance to go bad. Because if I go bad, everything I don't even let myself think now would come pouring out of me.

There are no pots left to wash, but I can't just sit here. I have to get up. Get back to work.

There is something else I could do. I get the broom bristles and head to the sitting room. There are still some chicken bones from the wedding feast stuck way back beside the sofa leg. If I just push myself under this sofa a bit more I can reach them.

There. I did it. Now she should be happy.

There's really nothing left to do now but wait. So I wrap my porani around me and hug my knees.

That's when I realize how quiet it is.

"Jameela." My father calls from the other room.

He's sitting on the sofa, leaning against the wall like he doesn't have the strength to sit up on his own. His glass is half full of that stinky stuff. The bottle has very little left.

"You need to get your things together," he says. "It's time to go." He doesn't look at me as he gets to his feet.

71

We're leaving?! I run to him and give him a big hug. At first he seems surprised. His arms are held out away from me, but finally he relaxes and hugs me back, real tight. And he spills some of his drink.

It doesn't take me long to pack. I don't have much. Just an extra set of clothes and my new comb. But *she* gave it to me. Maybe I should leave it here. No, I'll take it. Consider it payment for all the work I've done.

I bundle my things in my extra porani and make a loop as a handle so it's easy to carry.

Baba's calling again. I'd better hurry. I wouldn't want him to change his mind. We'll be all right. I wish Masood were here so I could say goodbye, but she sent him on some errand.

It's hard to keep up. Through this alley, round that corner, right, then left. In no time I've lost all sense of direction. The streets of Kabul are a maze. I'll never figure them out. It's been a long time since I've got out to walk. I'm gasping to catch my breath.

I can hardly hear what he's saying. Something about how things have changed. And did he say something about long ago in Arabia? My heart's pounding in my ears. All I can make out at the end of it is, "You know that?"

I nod, even though I have no idea what he was talking about.

He turns around again to continue walking, but he stumbles. I reach out to stop him from falling. He pauses, looking at me for a moment. Tears come into his eyes.

It's a glimmer of the way Mor used to look at me, and

hope fills my heart. Maybe things will really be different now.

He says, "You're a good girl. You'll be fine."

Insha Allah. Why is he talking like this? He sounds so strange.

And then he's walking again at that breakneck speed. Muttering something about opportunities and grabbing a chance at happiness while he can.

Is he questioning his decision to leave her? It can't be easy. She's so rich. We were guaranteed a home there. Now it will be tough again for a little while but I'm sure we'll be fine, as long as we have each other. He can count on me. I'll work hard. Maybe we can find another family to work for, better than the first place.

We get to a major intersection. Shops line the street. Little darkened huts all crammed together selling oranges and grapes and fabric and naan. There are cars, trucks, oxen, horses and people all jamming the road carrying things, going places, raising up dust to choke my throat and land on the fruit and fabric and naan. It's like that day we arrived here.

"Come, Jameela. Stand right here. I need to do something."

I grab hold of his sleeve.

"Where are you going?"

His face is twisted. He doesn't look at me. "Never mind."

I let go of his sleeve. He hitches up his shoulder to make his shirt fall properly. Then he takes five steps out into the crowd and does a strange thing. He looks back at me for a moment. For just a moment, our gaze is locked over the distance that separates us.

Then some people pass in front of me and when they move away, he's gone.

He's acting so strange. If I were taller I'd be able to see above people's heads and watch where he goes. I hope he doesn't take too long. But why did he tell me to wait here? He's always just dragged me along.

Maybe he saw that I was getting tired. It's good to rest. He didn't say I had to stand all the time, did he? But if I sit down maybe he'll pass by without seeing me. It can get very confusing here in the marketplace.

I'm nestled between two very dirty shops. There's a butcher to the right of me with cuts of meat hanging from the ceiling. On the left is a type of garage place with greasy automobile parts.

The butcher's shop has this strange kind of curled-up strip hanging from the ceiling near the meat. It's dotted with little black things. They look like bits of thread. I can't figure out what they are until a fly buzzes closer and then lands on the strip and gets stuck, adding one more speck to the strip. Fly carcasses.

The new fly victim is trying to get off. I see it push itself up, but it's hopelessly stuck. For a surprisingly long time it struggles. Then it stops, and for a moment I think it's dead. But the next time I look, it's trying again.

I hate flies, but dying that way just seems cruel. I'd rather smash it with a stick.

My feet start stinging after a while. I'll just sit down for a moment.

From this angle people look very tall. I've been indoors for so long that it's fun to just watch them rushing by with their parcels. They don't even glance at me, but sometimes their children do. They stare at me with big round eyes and pause for a moment, until their mother or father yanks on their arm and they get going again.

The shadow in the street starts to shrink. When we arrived, the shade stretched out over me halfway into the street. Now it barely covers my toes. It's going to be Zuhr time soon.

The butcher, a man with a big bushy moustache, comes out to stand at the doorway. He glances at me. I pull my porani in closer. He turns and goes back inside.

When will Baba come? He's taking so long.

My stomach growls so I give it a punch to settle it down. I wish I had some water to make wudu. Maybe I can ask the butcher. He looks like a nice man. But Baba's going to come soon, insha Allah. He can't be much longer. And what if I go back to make wudu just as he comes by and then we miss each other?

I'd better wait. I'm tired of watching the people, tired of checking each man's face to see if it belongs to Baba. All these people, I wish they'd get out of the way.

Where is my father?

The butcher has come out of his shop again, and this time he looks at me for a long time.

"Where did your father go, little girl?"

My stomach growls again so loud, I think he heard it. I sit up a bit straighter.

"I don't know." But I don't like the way that sounds so I add, "He's coming right back."

The man nods. "Well, if you need anything, let me know."

That was kind of him. A customer comes by. He calls the butcher Akram. They go back into the shop, and I hear them bargaining back and forth in a friendly way.

The day has got quite warm. The sun is angled down on me now. My mouth is dry.

When the butcher has finished with his customer he comes back outside again.

"You've been sitting there for a long time. I've made some soup. It's too much for me. Would you like some?"

I must refuse. He's just being polite. I open my mouth to say no, but other words come out.

"Yes, please. Tashakur."

He smiles so that his bushy moustache twitches upward, and in no time he brings me back a bowl. There are bits of onion and garlic and turnip, I think.

I need to lower my porani to eat it. He'll see my lip but there's nothing else I can do. I don't want to go into his shop. It would be too private. And what if Baba came while I was away?

I turn my back to the crowds so my face is somewhat hidden. When I've finished, I look up to see the man watching.

He smiles widely. "Oh, look how fast you ate that. Please have some more."

Even while I'm saying no, he brings the pot and spoons more into my bowl.

After the second bowl, he's about to pour a third, but I say, "No, please. I'm full." I think he can tell that I really mean it this time.

He glances at what's left in the pot and says, "Maybe we should save the rest for your father when he returns."

I have a feeling that this man hasn't eaten, so I tell him, "No, please. Go ahead and eat. I'm not sure when he's coming back."

He starts drinking right out of the pot and I realize that I must have been using his bowl. My face is hot. Why didn't it occur to me before?

He swirls the soup in the pot, not looking at me, and says, "So where is your mother?"

"Dead."

He nods and takes another sip. There's a bit of soup dripping from the ends of his bushy moustache. I cover my face to hide my smile.

"I know every vendor in this market. What was your father looking for? I'll tell you where he probably went."

"I don't know. He didn't say. Maybe he was looking for a job or a house. We just left our old place."

He's watching me with a strange look on his face.

"Well, we'll just wait and see then. I need to go pray Zuhr. Call me if a customer comes by."

I nod. "I need to pray, too."

I feel like I said the right thing. The man smiles and says, "I'll bring out my mat for you. You can make wudu at the back of my store. There's a washroom there."

I feel nervous about going to the back of his store. Mor always said that if a girl is alone with a man who is not closely related by blood, then the third with them is shai-tan.

"Agha, is it okay if you just bring out some water for me to make wudu out here?"

The man looks at me for a moment. I wonder if he's offended. He must realize I don't quite trust him.

Then he nods. "Of course. I'll bring some right away."

Everything inside me is telling me this man is okay, but still. His mat has pictures of the Kaaba and Medina mosque on it. It's very fine, but it's been used a lot. I can tell by the worn spots where his hands and knees have rested, a good sign. I pray my Zuhr right there on the street. It isn't hard. People don't bump me or anything. In fact they go out of their way not to disturb me.

Every so often the butcher comes out to check on me.

"Has he come yet?"

I shake my head. I wish he'd stop asking.

The shadows are beginning to grow on the other side of the street. The traffic isn't as thick as before.

Where could Baba be? Whatever he had to do couldn't have taken him this long. Did he forget about me? He was pretty drunk. But even drunk, how do you forget your own daughter? Maybe he's been in an accident. Maybe he's lying somewhere bleeding to death.

Maybe.

By the time the shadows have reached across the road

and are starting to chill my feet, the butcher is pulling down the metal grill that will lock up his shop.

He's looking at me with pity in his eyes.

"Still not back?"

I drop my head onto my knees so he can't see my watery eyes.

"You can't stay out here all night. Why don't you come home to my family? My wife has made some supper, and you're just about my daughter's age."

"But what if he comes while I'm gone?"

He looks up and down the street, squinting into the setting sun.

"I don't think he's going to come now. If he comes, he'll come tomorrow. And we can be back here early in the morning." He pauses.

What if it's a trap? What if this man is only pretending to be kind and all along is planning to lure me into some bad situation? I've heard of things happening, especially to girls.

But then I doubt they'd want to do anything to me. Not with my lip and all.

"Little girl, you can't stay here tonight. It isn't safe."

He's right. I ask Allah for guidance. Should I go with him? My heart feels calm and easy about it. He just doesn't feel dangerous.

I get up and grab my bundled-up porani.

"Okay, I'll come."

He takes me down one street and along another. I pull threads out of my porani to leave a bit of a trail, so I can

79

find my way back to that street if I have to. I wish I'd done that this morning when we were leaving her house.

After a while we get to a shop with a doorway on the side. He unlocks the door and leads me up a flight of dark, dirty stairs. I'm a few steps behind him. If he turns on me, I can run back down the stairs and get away.

But he doesn't turn, and instead he opens a door and three little boys and a girl my age jump at him with joy. Behind them is a nice-looking lady.

When the children see me they stare with their mouths hanging open. The lady, his wife, glances at him, then recovers and says, "Welcome."

It's while he's telling his wife what happened to me that the tears really start coming. Their daughter's name is Tahira. She brings me a tissue. It's soaked in no time.

After supper, I help Tahira with the dishes and cleaning up, trying to do as much as I can.

The lady keeps telling me I'm their guest and I don't have to do all that, but I insist. They've been so kind.

Then we pray Isha and we're sent to bed in a tiny room. The girl's asleep in no time. I could poke her and she wouldn't wake up. She's lying there on her back, open to the world.

I can't remember the last time I slept like that. For the longest while I've been curling up as tight as I can, with my knees tucked in, right up to my chin. It's the only way I feel safe.

I curl up and try to make myself drowsy but sleep won't come. Maybe it's the bed. It's so soft and comfortable. Can it be that I'm used to the floor?

80

I'm careful when I get out of the bed, even though it doesn't seem like anything would wake Tahira.

I curl up with my back to the wall and feel a bit better, but I still can't sleep. Maybe it's that I can't help worrying about my father. I can just picture him hitching up his shirt that last time so it fell right.

And that's when I realize.

When we left her house, I had all my things, but Baba's hands were empty. He hadn't taken anything of his own.

9

MAYBE he went back to get his belongings. But then why would it have taken so long?

I go through a thousand different reasons why he never came back, but none of them makes any sense. Except one.

What was he saying while we were rushing through those streets? I could barely hear him. Wasn't it something about ancient Arabia? Was he talking about what they did to the girl children back then? Was he saying at least he wasn't going to do that to me?

What am I going to do? Where will I live?

If I clean up this apartment before they wake up in the morning, maybe these nice people will let me stay.

What's wrong with me? I sound so stupid.

Why would they need me to clean when they have Tahira? They're not rich. They wouldn't need a servant.

If only I could read. People pay for their children to learn Quran. If I could teach their kids then maybe they would let me stay.

What will I say to Agha Akram in the morning? What can I say?

This little house has such a different feel to it. The silence isn't empty like at the first place, and it isn't cold like at *her* house.

It's a soft darkness. Peaceful.

The next thing I know I'm being tapped on my arm. In the gray dimness I can see the shadowy shape of Tahira.

"Wake up, sleepy. It's Fajr time."

The whole family's awake. Khalaa already has her porani on and is doing her sunnah. Even two of the little boys are awake. They've got their little kufis on. The hems of their pants are rolled up so I can see their tiny feet and knobby ankles. They're elbowing each other in the middle of their sunnah until Agha sees and pulls them apart.

They actually pray together as a family, like it's the most natural thing in the world.

I pray my sunnah with such a strange feeling growing in my chest. I don't know if I want to laugh or cry. I feel so fortunate to be here in this tiny apartment and I don't want this moment to end. If only it could stay like this forever.

When I've finished my sunnah, I wait beside Khalaa. Tahira's still praying. Khalaa catches my eye and smiles. And I really do feel welcome.

When Tahira's finished, we all stand up as one, without a word, and Ali, the oldest of the boys, says the iqama in a scratchy little voice.

There's something comforting about the practical way Tahira yanks off her porani and dumps it in a corner after we pray. Khalaa gets to her feet and takes the boys off to bed.

But Agha Akram opens the curtain and takes out a Quran. He reads by the growing light of dawn.

His lips move like they're silently saying the words.

I guess he senses me watching him because he looks up and says, "Are you all right?"

I nod. Mor used to recite Quran after Fajr. She taught me some of what she knew but we didn't get very far. First things were crazy with the bombings, and then she got too sick.

Agha Akram glances toward Tahira's room. "You can go back to sleep if you want. I don't mean to disturb you."

It feels as though I'm the one disturbing him. So I take the hint and leave.

I close the door gently. I wish I had the courage to ask him to show me what he was reading.

Tahira's already asleep. I curl up back in my corner.

The next thing I know I hear the footsteps of someone who's trying not to make noise and my eyes open. It's Tahira. She's carefully opening a dresser drawer, trying to get out some socks. She's wearing a school uniform complete with a matching hijab. Now I feel jealous.

There's a light knock on the door. Khalaa pokes her head in and whispers, "Is she awake?"

I sit up to show them I am.

She smiles at me. "Breakfast is ready."

It feels so strange to be served breakfast, not to have made it myself. We have milky tea with naan. The boys sit with their legs crossed, wearing their own little uniforms.

84

Agha Akram mutters the dua and takes a good-sized bite. While he's chewing he says, "Don't worry, Jameela. I'll go early to my shop and see if your father has come."

Should I tell him what I figured out? What if I'm wrong? What if Baba does show up? Better just see what happens.

My porani has slipped away from my face while I'm eating, and both of the boys are staring at me with big round eyes.

"What happened to your lip?" says Ali.

I quickly cover up my mouth.

Agha Akram gives Ali a nudge.

"But it looks so funny," Ali says. "What happened to it?"

Agha Akram glares at him.

It's hard for me to say, "I was born like this."

"Oh," says Ali. The other boys stare at me even more. Khalaa and Agha Akram look away. Tahira offers me another piece of naan. The food is good but I can't eat any more. My stomach feels too nervous.

I say, "Should I come with you, Agha?"

"If you'd like."

I'm wondering if I should leave my bundle of clothes here or take them with me. If I leave them here they might think badly of me, so I'd better take them.

I tidy up Tahira's room before I go. She left it a whirlwind mess of clothes and bedsheets.

Just as I'm leaving with her husband, Khalaa pats my head and kisses my forehead.

It feels so good to be touched.

"Tashakur for everything," I say, but the words sound

weak and useless. They would be fine if they'd passed me a spoon or brought me a cup of water.

Tashakur doesn't cover all they did for me. And yet saying too much more would be embarrassing.

She seems to understand and she nods at me. She's a very quiet woman, doesn't say much at all, but I can feel that it's all right with her.

In the street below I look for the little threads from my porani that I dropped to find the way back to Agha Akram's shop. The wind must have blown them away, or maybe some bird used them to line her nest. Anyway, I can't see even one so I guess I can feel better about not thinking of dropping threads when we left that woman's house.

It's so early that the other shops are still closed. I'm not surprised to see no one waiting by Agha Akram's shop. He looks disappointed. Is it because he's stuck with me for another day?

"Don't worry, Jameela. I'll ask around. They all know me. They'll keep an eye out for him."

I nod because I can't say anything. Something inside me is dead.

Agha Akram pulls up the metal grill that protects his store and goes inside. It smells like dried blood. He's not very tidy. There's a broom in the corner that looks like it's never been used.

Without asking I start sweeping out the shop. He objects, but I insist. I feel better to be doing something.

There are places on the wall where countless hands have left black marks. If I had a bucket of soapy water I

86

could wash them. I find one in the back, but the only soap is an old cake of hard yellow stuff. I don't think it will work.

"Please, Jameela. Leave that. It isn't necessary. We might as well go back home until midday. That's when business picks up."

The automobile mechanic shop is open. Agha Akram goes over to the man and starts speaking to him. I stand outside where I waited yesterday, chewing on the corner of my porani.

Agha Akram is waving his arms around while he's talking. He looks really angry. The other man glances over at me several times, shaking his head in pity.

Then the mechanic nods and presses a bill into Agha Akram's hand.

Agha says, "No brother, I don't need it."

"It'll help," he insists.

Agha tries to refuse several times. It's funny to watch them struggling back and forth trying to give each other the money. Finally the mechanic pats Agha on the back and calmly insists. Agha Akram puts it in his pocket and thanks him.

He says to me, "My neighbor will look out for your father. And he'll ask if any of the other vendors have seen him. You don't need to worry that you'll miss him."

Once we get around the corner, out of sight of the mechanic's shop, Agha Akram turns to me and says, "Can I trust you not to waste money?"

I nod.

"Here, then. You take this money that he gave me. You're going to need it. Don't spend it on foolishness. Keep it for emergency."

I hold the bill in my hand. It feels soft. I wonder how many hands it has passed through. There are letters and numbers on it. What do they say? I've never held more than a few coins in my life.

"How much money is this?"

Agha Akram looks at me like I just said a very stupid thing. I feel my face getting hot.

He takes the bill and points at the numbers in the corners. A circle followed by dots.

"That says five, then zero and another zero. Five hundred. This is five hundred Afghanis."

"Is that a lot of money?"

"About two days' wages! You keep it hidden. Don't let others see that you have it."

I tuck it away inside a fold of my dress.

I watch the route carefully, trying to memorize the twists and turns. It's not that hard. When we get back to the Akrams' place, Khalaa gets up to make some tea but I stop her and ask if I can do it.

Back and forth we argue like Agha Akram and the mechanic. Doesn't she realize that I don't like to be always on the receiving side?

Agha finally says, "It's okay. Let her do it."

Only the baby is at home. All the children have gone to school. Agha takes his wife inside their room and talks to her quietly. I think he's telling her the same thing he told the mechanic. Every now and then I hear Khalaa say, "Subhanallah!"

The baby keeps coming too close to the stove, two little gas burners on the ground. I've had lots of practice lighting them by now, but if that baby isn't careful, his clothes could catch fire. I turn my back so I'm blocking him.

When the tea is ready I take the two cups and stand outside the door of their room. I don't mean to eavesdrop, but I can't help it.

Agha Akram says, "Anybody could take advantage of her. She's too innocent. She didn't even know how much money I gave her. She'd be good for us. It wouldn't be that much more. She could be company for Tahira. She's a very good girl."

Khalaa says, "I know she's good, but it would be too hard. We'd have to send her to school. How can we afford it? It's already so much."

"We could manage. Each child brings their own baraka."

Khalaa says, "She'll be better off there. You know that. I'm not saying we'll never see her again. We can have her come to visit."

"Fatima, is it shaitan that's whispering in your ear? You know we should."

I can hear Khalaa stand up suddenly. What if she's coming to the door? She'll see me standing here, and the tea's getting cold. I knock then, and hear a quick movement inside.

"Come in," calls Khalaa.

"Here's the tea. I hope it's the way you like."

Khalaa smiles. "Tashakur, Jameela."

I nod and leave the room, closing the door behind me so I won't be tempted to eavesdrop. Mor always hated that kind of thing.

I sit with my knees pulled up to my chest, my porani wrapped around me. I can hardly breathe. I'm hoping so hard that Agha Akram will win the argument. Please, Allah, please, let them keep me. I'll never ask for another thing again.

Why wouldn't he win the argument? He's the man. He's the head of the house. It's his decision.

And yet. I'm afraid to hope.

I'll know by the way they come out of the room. If Agha is standing tall, then it will be yes. If Khalaa is smiling, then she'll have won.

The wait is unbearable. How much longer? I'm gnawing on my knuckles. Oh, please, Allah. I want this more than anything.

The corner of my porani is damp and frayed. I've chewed it so much my teeth ache.

Finally the door opens. It's Agha who is looking down at the floor. Khalaa's face is set and determined.

She won.

10

I'M NOT an orphan. I don't belong in an orphanage.

Agha Akram is talking to the khalaa in charge, telling her all about me. She's wearing a very thin porani, the kind Masood's mother wore. I wonder why these women even bother. They aren't covered. Their hair shows clearly through those flimsy things.

This new khalaa keeps glancing over at me and nodding. Then she walks over with a fake smile on her face.

"Welcome. Come, we'll find a place for you."

I have to go with her. Agha is looking at the floor, twisting his hands.

I take a deep breath and say, "Assalaamu alaikum, Agha. Tashakur for all you've done for me."

He wrinkles his nose. "I wish I could have done more." There's an awkward silence. I think we're both thinking of his wife. When the khalaa is busy he reaches into his pocket and presses another bill into my hands. Another five hundred Afghanis.

"You'll be better off here," he says. "You'll see."

I nod, even though I don't want to see.

"Come with me," says the khalaa. "We'll get you settled."

We walk down long halls with doors opening out to little rooms. I've never seen such beds. They're stacked, a bed on the bottom and another bed on top.

Where are the children? The real orphans.

The place is so big. I should pay attention to where we're going but somehow I can't. I don't care. I'd like to just crawl into one of those beds and fall asleep forever.

We go to a different section. In the last room at the end of a long hallway there's only one set of stacked beds. In the corner there's a whole bunch of junk. Rags and poles and things I can't recognize. And there are strange holes in the walls.

There are piles of sheets on the bottom bed. Khalaa puts them on the floor with the other things.

"You can have this bed. This really isn't supposed to be a bedroom, but it will have to do. You'll be sharing the room with one other girl. Her name is Soraya. She's in class right now but will be coming back soon." She glances at her watch. "They'll all be here soon. If you need anything just ask for me. You can call me Khalaa Gul."

This room is about as small as Tahira's. The stacked beds take up most of the space.

I lie down on the bottom bed. It feels so strange. What's underneath it on the floor? A bit of dust and dirt, but otherwise it's fairly clean. I grab one of the rags from the pile in the corner and wipe it out. There's more than enough room.

It feels nice to be tucked in here under the bed. It feels safe. Like a little cave. I like the way the steel mesh under the mattress above me looks. Little tufts of mattress bulge through the holes in the metal spring. I push at them with my finger but they pop right back out.

I must have fallen asleep because my eyes open all of a sudden when I hear footsteps slapping their way down the hall. Someone stops at the door, takes a running jump and lands on the bed above me. The wire mesh screeches, and the mattress bounces down so low it almost touches me.

I hug my bundle of clothes and hold my breath.

"She's not here yet!" the girl above me yells. "Come on in."

I see the bare feet of two other girls enter the room and they pile on top of my new bed.

"So what was all the screaming about?" one of the girls says.

The first girl says, "Khalaa Gul kicked those ladies out."

A small voice says, "But they were so nice. I like the doll they gave me."

Someone snorts.

Another voice says, "One of those ladies tucked me in one night. She took my blankets and put them all around me till I could hardly move. She made me repeat some words after her and then she put that doll in beside me. In the middle of the night it was poking me in the back so I threw it across the room."

"You know what those words were? The ones she was making you say?"

"What?"

"One of *their* prayers. And those things they nailed into

the walls were crosses. You know the little man on them? That was supposed to be Jesus."

Another voice says, "Alaihi salam."

"Yeah, Jesus, alaihi salam. They pray to those things."

The small voice says, "But why?"

"Never mind. They just do. Khalaa Gul found out what they were teaching us and she kicked them out. You should have heard her yell at them."

"But they were going to give us some shoes."

"You're going to sell your soul for some shoes?"

The others are quiet.

I'm scared to breathe. What if they find out I've been lying here on the floor listening the whole time?

Why didn't I lie on the bed? Now whatever I do I'll look so stupid. Maybe I should make a noise so they know I'm here.

Just then there's the sound of footsteps coming down the hallway. One of the girls says, "It sounds like her."

Two of the girls jump up and run to their own rooms. The one remaining gets off my bed and tidies the blankets.

It's Khalaa Gul. I can tell by her high-heeled shoes.

She says, "Soraya, where's the new girl? I left her right here."

"I don't know. I didn't see anyone."

I close my eyes and pretend to be sleeping. Khalaa Gul bends down and checks under the bed.

"There you are!"

Slowly I open my eyes and stretch. The stretch isn't all acting. She takes my hand and pulls me out.

"Soraya, this is Jameela. I want you to show her around and make her feel welcome. She's had it hard."

Soraya is a lot older than me, and she looks annoyed. I haven't begun things in a good way.

Khalaa Gul says, "Show her where the bathroom is and you girls wash up. It will be lunch time soon." Then she leaves.

Soraya says, "Why didn't you tell us you were under there?"

For a moment I'm tempted to lie and say I was sleeping.

"I'm sorry. I didn't know what to do. You just came in so suddenly. I really was sleeping."

I think it's the right thing to say. She nods, then looks at me more closely.

"Why are you wearing your chador like that in here? We're all girls, you know."

I take a deep breath and lower it so she can see my whole face. While I explain how I was born with my lip like this, I wonder if she'll make fun of me. Soraya nods as I'm telling her, and then she says something that surprises me. I thought she was the really tough kind of girl.

"Don't worry about it. It doesn't look that bad. I've seen worse." She turns and calls, "Zeba! Come here."

Zeba is about my age, with greenish brown eyes. Another girl comes with her. I recognize her feet. She must belong to the small voice. She's holding a scruffy little doll. She's tiny, with a small pinched dirty face and a runny nose. Her dress has stains on it, and her feet are grubby.

What is she doing with these bigger girls?

Zeba says, "Nobody asked you to come, Arwa. Why don't you play with girls your own age?"

Arwa shrugs. "They don't like me."

I'm not surprised. It's probably because she's so dirty.

Soraya nods her head toward me. "Seems as though we had a mouse listening."

Arwa holds her doll closer. "Mouse? Where?!"

Zeba gives her a shove.

"She's talking about her." She nods at me, too.

"Oh."

Soraya says, "This is Jamillah."

"No. Jameela." I emphasize the Arabic pronunciation.

Zeba laughs. "Who named you that?"

"My mother."

Zeba is still smirking. "Doesn't it mean pretty?"

I nod.

Zeba says, "Must have been a joke."

This time Soraya looks annoyed.

"Stop it, Zeba." To me she says, "Come, I'll show you the bathroom. It's broken, so most of us just go outside."

We head down the hall and quickly pass by the stinky washroom. Soraya introduces me to hundreds of girls. There's something about the way she says, "This is Jameela, she's new here," that puts all those girls on guard. They glance at my lip, and then they glance at Soraya, and then they just say, "Assalaamu alaikum," without making fun of me at all.

It's amazing. She knows all their names. Some treat her with respect. Others look afraid and a few look hateful. She must be the top of them all.

Zeba tags along. So does Arwa. Zeba seems to be in a bad mood. Arwa tries to hold her hand several times but she gives her a shove.

Anyone else would take the hint, but Arwa's the dumb kind of kid who keeps trying.

Now we're standing outside the meal area waiting. I feel something tickling my hand and look down to see Arwa trying to hold it. She looks up at me with big eyes like she's trying to be cute. I hate it when kids do that.

I know I should be kind, but she's so dirty, I just want to get away from her. Besides, it's a cruel world. She'll have to face that sooner or later.

So I pull my hand away.

Soraya says, "Make sure you're always at the head of the line. The first ones get the best pick."

I nod. "What will we be having?"

"Lunch is always the same. Yogurt and naan."

We all file in. The room is swept and clean. There are dusterkhans laid out neatly on the floor. Soraya scans the bowls and naan and quickly finds a few that have a bit more. She gestures to the three of us to come.

When the girls start eating, it gets very quiet. No one talks. Every girl is completely absorbed in lifting each bite to her mouth. There are the sounds of chewing, and the little smack of fingers being licked clean, but no words.

Zeba has finished her yogurt and still has a piece of naan. She reaches over and dips it in Arwa's bowl. Arwa looks up, frowns, but doesn't say anything. What can she say?

Zeba smiles at me like it's all just a big joke. Arwa's just a

97

little kid. She's not important. I don't even like her. It would be better to be on good terms with Zeba. I should smile back, but I can't. I look away. I can feel Zeba's eyes on me, but I don't care.

Later, Soraya comes to our room.

"They're going to put you in Arwa's class."

Class? School? Like Tahira and Farzana? I'm so excited, but then I check myself. Soraya makes it sound like I should be mad that I'll be in the little kids' class, but I'm not.

I have to wait until morning. How will I ever sleep?

Soraya steps on my mattress and hops up onto the bed above.

"It won't be that bad. Catch up soon so you can join our class."

I have to sleep on the bed or Soraya will think I'm strange. I huddle up to the wall. It's really quite comfortable as long as my back is covered.

Another strange place with new sounds that I need to get used to, and now I have time to think.

I wonder what Baba's doing. What did Masood say when he found out I was gone? How would they explain it to the relatives and neighbors?

How could Baba do this to me?

No.

Do not get angry. Do not get angry. Do not get angry.

Mor would be happy I'm going to school. Even if it is in Arwa's class. I'm so excited! I can't wait.

11

I'M ON a busy street, the same street with Agha Akram's shop. I see him standing at the front in a clean apron, his arms crossed. I wave but he doesn't recognize me.

Men and women flow past me. I can barely see their faces. They don't look at me but their elbows and shoulders jostle me. They are all traveling the wrong way and somehow I must get through. There's something ahead I must see, and yet I'm not sure what it is.

Through the crowd, I catch a glimpse of the back of Baba's head. I'm trying to get close to see if it's really him but he's walking quickly. It's hard to get through.

Then Baba turns to say something to someone beside him. It's her!

Such a rage boils up inside me. I push my way out to the edge of the crowd, see a good clod of cow dung lying on the ground and pick it up.

It's easier to make my way along the edges of the crowd. I'm right alongside them. I want them to see me. To know it's me. So I call them.

99

They turn in slow motion and with all my might, I hurl it at her. But he steps in the way.

It shatters all over Baba's face. Dung clings to his hair, his nose,¹ his clothes. And she's standing beside him as clean as ever.

It was supposed to hit her.

I can't stand. I fall in a heap, stepped over and stepped on by the crowd. Don't they feel me beneath their feet? Don't they know I'm here?

I wipe my eyes and they really are wet. I'm all curled up but it's not the street, it's my bed.

Even in my dream he chose her.

Mor was wrong. Being good isn't enough. You have to be beautiful or at least rich.

And despite the Prophet's advice (peace be upon him), I am angry. So angry I'm trembling.

The tears flow, and for once I can't stop them. They're so hot they could burn me. They make my pillow damp. Some even trickle into my ear.

I try to muffle my sobs. I don't want to wake Soraya. I don't want to talk about it. I just want to forget.

And when my eyes are all puffy and swollen and I just can't cry any more, what has changed? What have I solved? Nothing. Anger is for people who can do something about it.

When I stop sobbing, my heart is calm. And when I open my puffy eyes I can see that the light has changed. Dawn is on its way.

Fajr time. I'm ready to pray.

The water is cold and refreshing on my hot face. During

prayer I turn all my problems over to Allah. He has all the power. It's up to Him to take care of me.

Afterwards I go back and lie on my bed. I turn my pillow over so the damp side is away from me. I don't think I'll sleep, but before I know it, Soraya's calling me for breakfast. It's yogurt and naan again.

Afterwards we head off to our classrooms.

I'm so lucky. They give me a small piece of a pencil and a bit of paper. The paper's a little crumpled but one side is still clear. The rest of the kids in Arwa's class have nothing to write on.

I'm the biggest girl in the room.

Arwa sidles up to me so her bony knee is touching mine. She stinks so I move away. She slides closer again. I stare at her in such a way that it crushes the smile on her face and makes her look down.

I know it's mean but I can't help it. If only she wasn't so dirty. I can't stand filthy kids.

The teacher's name is Khalaa Kareema. She walks in smoothly wearing what these girls in Kabul call a chadri or burka. It's a long cloak that's tight at the head but flows out over your clothes, with mesh over the eyes.

Underneath she's holding books to her chest. She sets them down and then in front of us all, she takes off the chadri, folds it neatly and sets it aside. Her hair is braided at the back, her eyes are lined with kohl, slightly slanted. She sits down gracefully, settling her Punjabi clothes around her in a pretty manner.

Two of the girls are fighting. She just watches them for a

moment. Something makes me get up to try to pry them apart. One of them has a fistful of the other's hair and is pulling like she's enjoying it. I give that one a pinch. It's enough to make her let go.

Khalaa Kareema asks me to set the girls on opposite sides of the room. She has a chalkboard behind her that looks like it was once black but is now a dusty gray.

She starts with the alphabet. I already know some of the letters. I recognize *jeem* right away. She asks us to repeat after her. My voice is the loudest.

She shows us the vowel marks and how they change the sounds the letters make. It's like a secret code. It's so fascinating. I think I can get it. There's a letter for almost every sound you can make. And it's just a matter of stringing together the right letters and the right vowel marks to say whatever you want them to say. She's teaching us Farsi, but it wouldn't be hard to use the same letters to write what I want in Pushto.

At lunch time I seek out Soraya. I'm so excited. I have to share what I've learned with someone! Arwa's too little and Zeba wouldn't care.

But when I tell Soraya about it she snorts, "What are you talking about?"

"Learning to read!"

Soraya snorts again. "It doesn't make you a better person. If you're mean before you'll still be mean after. I know plenty of idiots who can read."

I make myself nod and keep my mouth shut. She finds the best bowls and naan and the four of us sit down. How can she not see what it means to me?

Arwa is trying to eat her food as fast as she can. There are drips of yogurt falling from her chin. Disgusting.

"Slow down." I tell her.

She doesn't say anything. She just licks her lips and glances at Zeba.

When we've finished, Zeba starts saying bad things about their teacher and Soraya laughs. I try not to listen, using my last chunk of naan to wipe my bowl clean.

Without warning, the door opens and Khalaa Gul leads a number of huge men inside. I'm the only one to grab my porani to cover my head and face.

They're foreigners, soldiers, wearing splotchy dull green uniforms. I wonder if they are American. I wonder if they are the ones who killed my family.

They're standing there in their huge black boots, so tall they practically touch the ceiling.

Khalaa Gul gestures in our direction and says something in a strange language. Soraya nudges Zeba, and they both bend their heads and giggle.

I nudge Soraya. "What?"

"Khalaa Gul is at it again. You'll see."

All the other girls are quiet. There's a nervous silence in the air. Khalaa Gul comes right up to me and touches my chin to lift my face toward these strange men.

What is she doing? What's happening? She's talking to them in that strange language. They're staring at me. I want to hide. She grabs a corner of my porani and tries to pull it away. I yank it from her.

Then she bends down and whispers in my ear, "These

103

men could help you. You need to show them your face."

The whole room is staring at me, including Soraya and Zeba. I've got no choice.

Khalaa Gul says, "It's all right, Jameela. I'm right here."

So I let the porani fall away. But that's not enough. Khalaa Gul grabs my chin and lifts my face right up so they can see my ugly lip.

I might as well be standing there naked. That's how I feel. I'm forced to stare right into their glassy blue eyes. They're looking at me with pity on their faces.

Khalaa Gul finally lets go of my chin and I can get away from their strange faces and piercing eyes. They say something, and Khalaa Gul looks happy. She nods vigorously. Some of her hair escapes from that flimsy porani she wears and swishes back and forth.

They stand there for I don't know how long, talking about us in this other language, like we don't even exist.

Then she goes down the room and points out a few more girls.

Arwa touches my arm. "Are you all right?"

My face is hot.

Soraya nudges me. "Jameela?"

"I'm all right." I feel a bit better when I pull my knees up to my chest and hug them.

Soraya says, "Don't worry about it. It's happened to all of us. You just have to get used to it. She brings all these foreigners through here and tells them our sad stories so they'll give the place money. It's how we survive."

Zeba nods. "And then she gets mad at them for something and kicks them out. She's always going through new people. These men might actually be useful. I wonder if they'll fix the toilets?"

Arwa touches my hand again. "Don't feel bad. I was scared, too, the first time it happened. I'm much bigger now."

Her words make me smile. Then she says, "I'm glad you're in my class. Do you like my teacher?"

I stiffen and turn away. She's trying to trick me. Make me like her. She's too clingy. There's just something about her.

After lunch we pray Zuhr. I'm shocked at the way the girls pray. Most of them don't even bother to say the words. Soraya prays, but Zeba sits in a corner and chats with a friend.

There are some books in here. I pick one up and look at the squiggles and dots and lines on the page. Some of them look a little familiar to me now. I'm sure I see *jeem*s and a few *ha*s and even a *kha*.

Khalaa Kareema sees me and comes over.

"Please be careful with these books. They're the only copies we have."

"I wouldn't ruin them for the world."

She looks at me like I've said something strange.

She says, "These are some Qurans and these are tafseers, translations and explanations of the Quran. Some are in Farsi and some are in Pushto. See the lettering?"

I touch the spines of the books.

"Will I learn to read these?"

"Insha Allah. It won't be too hard. Pushto and Farsi took the Arabic letters and just added a few extra. They are all very similar."

If I could learn to read these very books, Mor would be so proud of me!

Khalaa Kareema closes the book and says, "I'm glad you joined our class. I think the little ones will pay better attention now that you're here."

I nod. "If I can help in any way, let me know."

She smiles, and for a moment she looks less tired.

I'm scared to ask, but I know I shouldn't be.

"Khalaa, could you show me how to write my name? I saw it once very quickly, but I can't remember all the letters." I can't help thinking of Masood and that woman.

Her face lights up.

"Of course! It's Jameela, right?"

"My grandfather brought the name back when he went for Hajj. My mother was just a little girl and he told her if she ever had a daughter, she should give her that name."

Khalaa Kareema nods. "Yes, you pronounce it the Arabic way. It means beautiful."

As she writes it, just like Masood did, she says each letter it contains out loud. *"Jeem, meem, ya, lam, ha."*

One continuous word, not broken up at all. It really is beautiful.

12

I HEAR footsteps coming so I hide the book Khalaa Kareema gave me and sit up.

Soraya walks in.

"Good news! The soldiers fixed the toilets. Now they're working on the windows and heater. They might even be fixed before the real cold hits." She motions at me to make room, and when I do she sits down beside me.

"It will be nice to be warm," I say.

She snorts. "First the soldiers break our country. Now they want to fix it."

I nod. I don't understand it either. These foreigners do what they please. They are powerful and we are not.

She turns to look right at me.

"What are you doing? You're always in here lying around. Something wrong?"

I think of the book that's bulging under my right foot.

"No, no. I'm okay. Just tired." I make myself yawn.

"When are you going to get out of Arwa's class? I told the other girls about you and they keep asking."

How can I tell her that I could have left a month ago? I like Arwa's class. I like Khalaa Kareema. I'm even taking the slower ones aside to help them learn, and in exchange, Khalaa Kareema keeps me after class and teaches me more things.

The next day Khalaa Kareema says, "So have you finished with that book I lent you? My son will be needing it soon."

I hold out the book. My fingers cling to it a bit even as she's taking it from my hand.

"How did you like it?"

"I didn't know the Prophet (peace be upon him) was an orphan."

Khalaa Kareema nods. "Just imagine. What he was able to do. And in that society! He would have been at their mercy."

"The way they lived, it kind of sounded like my village."

She smiles. "Yes, things haven't changed that much for some of us. Would you like me to teach you Arabic? There are more books in Arabic than in Farsi or Pushto. And the Arabic ones are more accurate. Some of the Farsi books get a bit...into fantasy."

"Fantasy?"

"They start adding a lot of imaginative things to the facts. I think the facts are good enough on their own. They don't need to dress them up."

I nod. Mor thought like that, too. Some of the mullaas in the village would say things about the Prophet (peace be upon him) that were impossible, like he didn't have a shadow because that way no one could step on it and insult him. Mor would get mad at them. She said it was almost as if they were turning him into something more than human.

Maybe that's why I like Khalaa Kareema so much. She reminds me of Mor.

"I would love to learn Arabic," I say.

She hands me another book. It's bound in red fabric. The edges are a bit worn and dusty. On the spine in gold lettering it says *Ar-Raheeq al Makhtoum.*

Khalaa says, "That means 'The Sealed Nectar.' It's supposed to be the best out of Arabia these days. The most accurate. All the ulema say so."

"Is it another biography?"

"Yes. It's good to read many different ones. Then you can compare the way they describe the life of the Prophet (peace be upon him) and what each of them chose to focus on. Some focus on the Meccan period, others on the Medina period. You can learn from many of them." She adds, "This one's a Farsi translation."

She takes out her papers and starts planning for tomorrow and I start reading. A peaceful silence settles over the two of us. And underneath it — you can almost feel it in the air — is friendship. I really like her, and I think she likes me.

This is the best room in the orphanage. With all the peace and quiet it's easy to concentrate.

I should get ready for dinner. Soraya and Zeba will be waiting but I just want to read a bit more.

I feel a touch on my shoulder and look to see Khalaa Kareema smiling down at me.

She says, "I've never seen such an eager student. You make my job easier."

Sudden tears blur my eyes. What's wrong with me? She said something nice. I should be happy instead of dripping like a tap.

She rubs my shoulder and bends closer.

"Are you all right?"

My face is hot. I must stop.

I take a big gulp and wipe my eyes hard. I will stop this nonsense.

"I'm all right."

The door bursts open and Khalaa Gul is there with one of the soldiers. Khalaa Kareema and I rush to cover ourselves, but Khalaa Gul brings the soldier right up to me and orders me to show my face. I have no choice.

This time the man actually touches me. He's rather ugly, but not because there's anything wrong with him. He's got hardly any hair, his skin is gray like paste, and he has a stubbly beard.

He holds my chin and moves my head up to see my lip, then he pushes his grubby finger against my lip.

"Open your mouth," says Khalaa Gul.

So I do.

He takes out a flashlight and shines it up to the roof of my mouth.

He says something over his shoulder to Khalaa Gul, and she looks pleased. They talk back and forth in that foreign language and then the soldier stands up straight. He says something more. It's so strange the way they can

110

say things to each other that mean nothing to me.

I wish I could speak all the languages. Maybe if I watch and listen closely enough I can pick up what they're saying, but at the end of their conversation I still feel completely muddled.

He says a few more things, nods twice at Khalaa Gul, nods at Khalaa Kareema and leaves the room, his boots sounding loud in the hallway.

Khalaa Gul rushes over to me.

"Oh, Jameela, such good news! That was an army surgeon! He's going to fix your lip. He says it's just cleft, a small problem, easy to fix."

My lip can be fixed?

I don't know what to say.

Khalaa Gul pulls back a little and watches my face.

"Is everything all right? Don't you want your lip to be fixed?"

Something in me wakes up.

"Oh, yes! I've never wanted anything more." My words shock me. They just burst out of me.

Khalaa Gul nods. "Good. They're going to come for you tomorrow. I'm going with you so no need to fear."

She turns on her heel and walks out the door.

Khalaa Kareema steps forward, her eyes shining and all crinkled up.

"I'm so happy for you! It couldn't happen to a nicer person." She pulls my porani from my face and says, "Oh my, you'll look so nice with it done."

I give her a hug. She has to get home to her family so she

111

packs up her things and goes, and I'm left alone to think about what I said.

I've never wanted anything more? Really?

What about wanting to stay with Agha Akram's family? What about wanting Mor to get well?

What a selfish thing to say. Will I become like Soraya's friends who huddle around the mirror in the bathroom trying to catch a glimpse of their faces?

It's starting to get dark outside. I can see my reflection in the window. I go up close and pinch the two open sides of my lip together. If they were sewn up, my face would be perfect. I feel myself getting excited.

When I tell Soraya she says, "What?! Are you crazy?"

Zeba nods. "How can you trust those soldiers? They kill for a living."

"Don't you have any dignity?" Soraya says. "I hate how we go begging to these foreigners for every little thing. I had an aunt who was operated on and she died even while they were cutting her. It's very dangerous. Much better to live with something like that than take a chance. It doesn't even look that bad."

Zeba agrees.

Why are they saying these things? If they had a chance like this wouldn't they grab it?

"Khalaa Gul said it was easy to fix. I don't think it's risky at all. These foreigners know about these kinds of things."

Soraya shakes her head. "You're making a big mistake. It's a trap. He could just want to get you alone so he can do what he wants to you."

Zeba adds, "A deadly mistake."

He didn't seem wicked and Khalaa Gul sounded so positive when she said it was a small problem.

I try to sound as confident as I can. "It will be fine, insha Allah. You'll see."

They keep trying to convince me not to do it, but soon we're let in to eat and they're too busy with their food to keep insisting. But right after supper they start back again.

Finally I turn to Soraya and say, "Thanks for being so worried about me, but I think I'm just going to go ahead and do this."

Soraya and Zeba glance at each other.

Zeba says, "Okay. I guess she just thinks she knows everything. We should just leave her alone to do what she wants."

"Yes. I can't believe we even bothered."

They turn and start walking away. I run after them.

"No, please. Soraya, Zeba. You don't understand."

Soraya turns then, "What do you mean I don't understand? I understand a lot more than you! I'm older and I've been around longer! I know exactly what happens around here. I make it my business to know what's going on, and I'm telling you, you're making a big mistake. You're walking into a trap!"

She and Zeba stand there for a moment waiting. If I don't listen to them things will never be the same between us. I just know it.

What would Mor want me to do? That's easy. She would tell me to have the operation.

"I really appreciate your worrying about me, but I'll be all right, Soraya. You'll see."

Soraya makes a face. They turn, leaving me standing there in the hallway.

All that night Soraya won't talk to me. She goes to sleep without replying when I say good night. I never realized how comfortable her chatter made me feel. I guess I should be feeling bad, but a little part of me is getting stubborn about it.

Why should she make such a fuss just because I've made up my mind to do something and she doesn't approve? What's it to her?

The darkness feels very lonely.

Thoughts of the surgery and Soraya and Zeba and the new biography of the Prophet (peace be upon him) I'm reading keep winding around in my head all night. Every few minutes I wake up and listen to the sounds of the orphanage, trying to figure out if it's Fajr time.

Finally I wake up to that gray dimness and I know it's time to get up. I feel like I never slept.

I pray Fajr with all my heart, asking Allah to watch over me.

Khalaa Gul comes for me before breakfast. I'm not allowed to eat because of the surgery. A different soldier arrives to take me. He looks tired. I wonder if he had a bad night, too.

We walk out to the courtyard, where there's a dirty green army vehicle waiting. This time I sit in a chair with a belt fastened across my lap. The soldier clicks it into place for

114

me. I look at the buckle. Such a tiny machine, with only one job, to keep you in place. These foreigners have all kinds of gadgets I've never seen before.

Khalaa Gul is in the front, chattering away to the man. Fawning over him like a beggar. I see what Soraya means. And the worst thing is, she flutters her hands while she talks, pulling her flimsy porani up every time it slips off her hair and giggling whenever she answers a question.

Isn't she married? Why is she talking to this man in such a shameless way?

It's different driving in an army car. People look at you strangely. They rush out of the way like chickens afraid of being run over.

We drive for quite a bit until we get to a high-walled camp. There is a guard with the same splotchy green uniform and helmet. In his arms is a massive rifle. It's black and coated with dust from the street. He sees the man who's driving and waves us through.

Inside there are more white people walking around in short-sleeved shirts and army uniforms. They hardly look at us.

Then I'm taken into an area with different tents. On the front there's a big red mark on a white background. It looks a bit like an *alif* with a line across it. A lady presses a round black thing to my chest that has tubes that go into her ears. I think she's listening. Then she puts a black thing around my arm. She pumps it up and it squeezes me tight, then it slowly loosens. She also puts a white glass stick in my mouth. Khalaa Gul tells me not to bite it but it's hard.

Somehow I want to. They place it under my tongue and I have to keep it there for a while. I still haven't seen that man from yesterday.

I have to lie down on a strange narrow bed and uncover my face. The lady's face is inches away from me, but she's not looking into my eyes. She's concentrating on my lip. She's wearing glasses and I can see myself reflected in them. I look small and scared. Behind the shine of the glass, her eyes are a brownish green.

Then she puts a black kind of mask thing on my face and Khalaa Gul tells me to breathe deeply and count to ten.

The last thing I remember is the number six.

13

SOMEONE is calling me but I just want to sleep. I snuggle down into the blankets. There's a light touch on my forehead. I brush it away.

Someone says something in a strange language. Khalaa Gul answers. She's standing at the side of my bed talking to a nurse. Then she turns toward me.

"Ah, you're finally awake! Come now, we need to go home. We've bothered these kind people long enough."

There's something about these blankets. They're warmer than usual. I hate to leave them. The nurse takes me by the arm and slowly lifts me up until I'm sitting. My mouth feels numb. I touch the side where it used to be open, but it's covered in a bandage.

Khalaa Gul says, "Leave the dressing alone. It has to heal now."

The same nurse takes my arm and helps me swing my legs over the side of the narrow bed. She says something that I think means slowly. I'm a little wobbly, like a newborn lamb.

Khalaa Gul takes my arm and leads me back to the army

truck. She makes a huge fuss over me in front of the army people. It makes me feel embarrassed. I climb into the vehicle slowly and sink down into the seat. It feels so good to sit down.

We drive through Kabul on the way back to the orphanage. I wish I could see the Akrams' shop. I wish Baba or Masood could see me riding like this.

We're back at the orphanage too soon. As soon as the army people are gone, Khalaa Gul seems to lose all interest in me. She calls a girl standing by the office to help me to my room. It takes a long time to walk down those hallways.

When I get to my bed, I'm grateful to lie down. Luckily Soraya's in class. I want nothing more than to sleep.

I wake up when I hear noise in the corridor. What will Soraya say? She'll be so angry I defied her.

Little feet come running up first. Arwa jumps onto my bed and peeks at me through the blankets.

"Can I see your lip?"

I push her away a bit too roughly and she falls off the edge of the bed. I feel bad when she cries out but not bad enough to get up to help her.

Soraya comes in and says, "What are you doing to the poor child?" She scoops up Arwa and makes a big fuss of comforting her. It's an act. I know it. She must find her just as annoying as I do.

Arwa's eyes are closed and her face is pressed against Soraya's chest. If she were a kitten, she would be purring.

I want to turn my back to the door. Shut them all out of my view.

Before I can turn over Soraya says, "Let me see the damage."

It's an order. At least she's talking to me. Zeba leans closer like she wants to see, too.

I push down the blanket from my nose.

"I'm not supposed to uncover it yet."

"Nonsense! Let me see."

So I sit up and show them my lip.

Soraya touches the dressing and picks at the tape at the corners.

"Don't!" I say, but she keeps at it.

Soraya manages to lift a corner of the tape. My lip isn't as numb any more. The stickiness of the tape pulls at my skin as she lifts it. It feels as if it's being snapped by a hundred rubber bands. The dressing is stuck fast. The blood must have soaked through and dried.

Soraya tugs at it but I pull away.

"No, don't. You'll make it bleed."

"Fine! Be like that." She turns, calls Zeba to her side and walks out.

The only one left is Arwa. She's sucking her finger, staring at me. I make a face at her, and wince when it hurts. She takes the hint but just as she leaves, she glances at me over her shoulder. It's a look of reproach and it stings more than my lip.

How come I can put up with everyone in here but her? She's just so dirty, but I know it's not that. There are others much dirtier.

I turn my back to the door and try to settle down to sleep, but I'm much too wide awake now.

They've gone for lunch. This will be one time the tiny mirror in the bathroom won't be crowded.

There's no one in the hallway. I'm glad my bare feet make no sound. I peek around the corner. The way is clear, down another hallway.

Why am I being so sneaky? I'm just going to the bathroom.

The mirror is small and high up. I have to stand on tip-toe to see the bottom of my cheek. With my tongue I can feel the stitches that run all the way through, inside the top of my lip. I lift the corner of tape that Soraya was working on but the dressing really is stuck.

I might as well go back to bed. But my stomach is grumbly. I haven't eaten since yesterday. Maybe I should go to lunch, too. I feel pretty good. They didn't say I couldn't eat afterward. I'll just make sure I chew on the other side, away from the stitches.

When I enter the lunch room, all the girls look up from their yogurt and naan. Most of them smile when they see me. There's a kind of cheer that goes around the room.

Khalaa Kareema says, "Jameela! I was just going to check on you. How are you feeling? Come, sit here. Girls, make room."

Soraya's way on the other side with Zeba and Arwa. That's my usual spot but somehow I don't feel like picking my way over there. I'm tired from all the walking. It's nice to settle down right here.

Khalaa Kareema goes into the kitchen and brings out another bowl with some naan.

"I saved this for you. Can you eat? Would you like me to

break the naan into pieces and soak it in the yogurt so it's soft?"

I smile, then wince with the pain it causes. My lip is definitely not numb any more.

"It's all right. I'll do it."

I break up the naan and drop it into the yogurt. Fyma, a girl next to me, says, "How was the operation? Were you scared?"

"A little."

Another girl beside her says, "Did the soldiers point their guns at you?"

I frown. "No."

"What kind of knife did they use?"

"I didn't see the knife."

Khalaa Kareema hands me a spoon and I stir the yogurt to soften up the naan.

Another girl says, "I would be terrified!"

"I was a little scared. I heard things," I say, and I can't help glancing in Soraya's direction. "But it was okay. There was a nurse. She was nice."

They lean closer while I tell them about the operation. Girls in the next row are turning around to listen. Soon there's a crowd around me. It feels so strange to be the center of attention.

I see Soraya glance at me a few times. Her face is neutral. Zeba scowls at me.

Arwa joins the group gathered around. Her nose is running all the way down to the edge of her lip and there's a bit of yellow crust around the edges.

She asks, "Did it hurt?"

Ugh! I'm losing my appetite, so I turn away and don't answer, but Fyma says, "Yeah, did it?"

"It didn't hurt right then, but it's hurting now."

I stir the yogurt again. The naan is nice and mushy. I can't answer all these questions and eat at the same time.

Finally Khalaa Kareema comes to my rescue and tells the girls to leave me alone.

They look so disappointed. I had no idea they were this friendly.

With my belly full I just want to go back to sleep, but it's Zuhr time. I make wudu carefully, trying not to get the bandage wet. Fyma and her friend Raisa splash some water on themselves, but they don't wash their hands and face and arms and feet three times. Why can't they make wudu properly?

Only some of the girls make the effort.

They all fuss over me. Fyma shoves some of the girls out of the way and ends up at my side.

By the time we get to the prayer room, I'm drained. I don't have the strength to stand up, so I sit in the corner with my back to the wall and pray sitting down.

Praying while sitting takes much less time, so I finish my sunnah before the others and have time to watch them. It amazes me how many girls sit on the sides and turn to each other to whisper and gossip. It makes me wonder what they say about me.

Soraya sees me sitting and says something to Zeba, who

nods. Maybe they think I'm being lazy sitting instead of standing to pray.

Raheema, one of the bigger rather homely girls, comes in from making wudu. The edges of her sleeves and her face are wet. And as she walks by I see that the back of her dress is caught in the drawstring of her pants. Her whole backside is exposed. Worst of all, her pants are wedged into the crack of her bottom.

Fyma points at her and doesn't even try to muffle her laughter. She nudges her friend Raisa so she can see and laugh, too.

Poor Raheema. She has no idea why they're laughing. She just looks at the girls and smiles, trying to get in on the joke.

I wish I was closer. I'd yank her dress out so it would cover her shame.

Soraya looks up from her dhikr to see what all the girls are laughing at. When Raheema passes by, her eyes widen, but she doesn't laugh.

By this time Raheema is smiling and laughing along with everyone else. Soraya gets up, steps over a couple of little kids, grabs Raheema by the shoulder and yanks out her dress where it's trapped so it falls properly. A look of realization comes over Raheema's homely face. The other girls roar with laughter.

Beside me Fyma's laughing so hard she's wiping tears from her eyes. Raisa's laughing, Zeba's laughing. Even Arwa is laughing, but Soraya nudges her, says something and she stops.

The only ones who don't laugh are Soraya and myself.

The iqama is called. Time for prayer to start. Poor Raheema. She looks so embarrassed and nobody's letting her into line. Soraya calls her forward and lets her stand between her and Zeba.

Fyma makes a nasty face at Soraya's back, and Raisa rolls her eyes. Fyma turns to me and says, "That stupid Soraya. She's always spoiling our fun."

After the prayer, Khalaa Kareema says I must go right back to my room and lie down. Some of the girls argue about who gets to take me, and Fyma manages to get the honor.

Up and down the corridors, she doesn't walk too fast and even offers her arm for me to lean on. I say, "Tashakur but I wouldn't want to burden you." It feels unwise to lean on her. Maybe she'll complain to the others about how heavy I am.

When we get to the room Fyma tucks the blankets in around my back so I'll be warmer.

She says, "You don't remember me, do you?"

I feel bad. "I'm sorry, but no."

Fyma smiles. "You helped me out. I was supposed to mop the kitchen but you did it for me, for three nights. I was sick. You don't remember?"

I shake my head. "Sorry."

She nods. "Well, there were a lot of girls you helped out."

I guess there were.

14

THE BANDAGES came off today. I'm surprised at how fast my lip has healed. There's only a thin red line to show where the surgeon joined the two sides together.

It's so strange to see my face whole. I can't help angling my head this way and that to check out my new look in the mirror.

Fyma gives me a nudge.

"Hurry up, Jameela. Let us have a turn."

Oh, dear. Am I turning into one of those silly girls? I vow not to spend so much time in front of the mirror, but I can't help sneaking a look even as I'm turning away. Just a quick little glance, like getting acquainted with a stranger.

I like what I see.

I'm fingering my porani. I should cover up my face, but for the first time I really don't want to. Is it so bad to want others to see my new face? Is it like bragging?

Wasn't I always looking down at them for showing off? Didn't I tell Masood that I would wear the porani even if I was beautiful? Especially if I was?

125

But they're all girls. I don't even need to wear it all the time. I only do so because the soldiers come in so unexpectedly.

I won't. I'll just leave it around my shoulders like everyone else.

It feels so strange not to have it on my head. I feel so naked.

Fyma finishes making her wudu and she comes up alongside me.

"We'd better hurry. The iqama's going to go soon."

We rush into the prayer hall. Soraya's way up ahead with Zeba. I put on my porani properly and start praying my sunnah. Before I even finish, the imam stands up to start the fard. I rush through the words to finish my prayer, but still they've gone down for the first ruku before I can join the jamat. I'll have to make up that rakat at the end of the prayer, after everyone's already finished.

I hate rushing like this. Oh, why did I dawdle in front of the mirror? I've never been so late for my prayer. Asthaghfirullah.

When I finally finish, it feels so normal to just leave the porani on my head. That's what I've always done. But now it's different. So I reach up and put it around my shoulders again.

My hair's a bit messy from the porani. I guess I'll have to make sure I keep it properly combed.

Fyma says, "You look so nice now! Better than Soraya." My face feels hot. I don't know what to say.

I should go. Khalaa Kareema is waiting for me, but for the first time I don't feel like helping out in her class. I'd rather be with girls my own age. Luckily Arwa hasn't gone

126

yet. She's skulking around the corners of the prayer hall, dawdling as usual.

I call her over. She runs up quickly.

"Tell Khalaa Kareema I won't be coming today. I'm going to go to the big girls' class now."

She's got her finger in her mouth. Such a dirty habit. But then she's such a dirty little girl.

Didn't she hear me? Why is she still standing there?

"Go on, Arwa! Tell her!"

Fyma glances at me quickly. I guess I didn't have to be that loud.

Arwa's face looks like a crushed-up tissue. She turns slowly and heads down to her class.

Never mind. She'll get over it.

It feels so strange coming into this big class. Girls give me looks and move over a bit to make room. Soraya glances at me but doesn't smile. Zeba scowls. The teacher, Khalaa Rasheeda, looks tired. The girls look bored.

Khalaa Rasheeda says, "Settle down, girls. Jameela, please hurry up and find a spot. I'd like to continue."

She's teaching them about the water cycle. Khalaa Kareema taught me that a while ago. The girls are restless. They're whispering. One girl is leaning against the wall, sleeping. Maybe if we had desks and weren't so crammed together on the floor, things would be better. Soraya doesn't even hide that she's chatting with Zeba.

Fyma leans over and says, "Look at Soraya! She thinks the sun wouldn't set without her permission."

I don't say anything.

Fyma tries again, "Most of the class hates her, you know. She's so bossy."

I nod. Soraya definitely is bossy.

Raisa is listening in on our conversation.

She says, "Oh, yes. I'm glad you're challenging Soraya. She's been a real pain in the neck."

I'm challenging Soraya?

Khalaa Rasheeda erases the board and says, "Now, who can tell me what I just showed you? When the rain falls what happens?"

Raisa calls out, "We get wet."

The other girls laugh. Khalaa Rasheeda frowns.

"None of that. I want you to raise your hands and answer politely."

This time Raisa raises her hand. Hers is the only hand up so Khalaa Rasheeda has to call on her.

"Do you know what happens when the rain falls, Raisa?"

"We get wet."

All the girls laugh again. Khalaa Rasheeda looks so annoyed.

I put up my hand.

"Yes, Jameela?"

"The water is absorbed by the land, runs off into streams and then goes back up into the air."

Khalaa Rasheeda looks relieved. Fyma, Raisa and some of the other girls send me disappointed looks.

When it's over, Fyma and Raisa get up together and leave me behind. The other girls are not jostling to be near me any more.

Somebody nudges past me. It's Zeba. She's walking quickly beside Soraya through the crowd of girls. Most see them coming and move out of the way.

I find myself heading down a familiar corridor. Khalaa Kareema is just leaving the classroom.

When she sees me she says, "I missed your help."

Without thinking I say, "I missed helping you."

She's watching me so intently it makes me squirm, and I realize that my porani is still down around my shoulders.

Instinctively I lift it back up to cover, but then drop it again. I won't cover just to please Khalaa Kareema.

"Will you be coming by tomorrow?" she asks.

"Yes. I think so."

For the rest of the day most of the girls don't bother with me at all. I'm kind of glad.

At night I crawl into my bed and turn my back to them. And for the first time since she died, I dream of Mor.

She's sitting straight and tall, kind of stiff, wearing very white Punjabi clothes and a porani. Her face is not covered, and she looks young and healthy.

The happiness at just seeing her is overwhelming.

I call, "Mor! Mor!"

She doesn't turn to look. I run around so I'm in her line of sight.

"Mor!"

She turns her head away. And I see then that I'm not wearing anything at all.

People are walking by, not even noticing that I'm standing there without anything on. I want to hide, but I can't leave her.

She won't look at me. She's staring at something in the distance. I keep calling her, getting more and more desperate.

I stamp my feet like a little girl. I stamp and cry and shout and scream, and she won't look at me. She keeps staring off at something else. Like she's made of stone.

I can feel the dream slipping away and I don't want it to. I'm grabbing at it but it's turning to shreds, wisps of smoke that disappear into the air.

There's nothing but blackness behind my eyes, and when I open them, there's the familiar grayness of dawn. Fajr time.

I uncurl my legs. The floor is ice. Soraya's still sleeping, but I think she'd want me to wake her up, so I give her a nudge.

She turns and looks at me.

"Oh, it's you."

"It's time for Fajr."

She sits up, rubs the grit in the corner of her eyes.

"Oh, all right. Tashakur."

I pad down the hall and make wudu. A few other girls are doing the same. I don't see Fyma or Raisa anywhere. Zeba's not there either.

There's something about the familiar washing of wudu that makes me feel better. More normal. I tie up my porani the way Mor taught me, and I enter the prayer hall. At this time of the day it's quiet and peaceful. Only the girls who are strong in their faith bother to get up.

Soraya comes in. She's looking around and then ends up picking a spot right next to me to pray her sunnah.

There's a Quran with tafseer in Pushto in the corner. I don't have to hide any more so I pick it up and start reading some verses.

When she's finished her sunnah Soraya sits so close to me that her knee touches mine. It feels good.

And when the iqama begins we stand side by side, girls in a line.

15

THERE HAS been a new crop of arrivals at the orphanage. Some of the girls have families so poor they left them here, but at least they come to visit now and again. And then there are the true orphans like Soraya, Zeba and Arwa. The only one who's been totally abandoned is me, and they all know it.

I can see it in their eyes when they pass me in the hallway, and I can see it in the way they pause in their whispering when I come into the prayer hall. Girls in groups of two, with their heads bent toward each other, looking right at me, talking out of the sides of their mouths.

Saying how could her father do such a thing? It's unnatural. What's wrong with her that he would do such a thing? What did she do to deserve it?

They'll stop after a while if I just leave them alone. If I pretend it doesn't bother me and keep my head high, they'll eventually stop.

The scar on my lip has faded. I look almost perfect. I

132

wish Baba could see me this way. Would he change his mind and want me back?

The soldiers fixed the heat and windows in time for spring, but now the fighting in the hills has intensified. The Americans are fighting another war, too, and the Taliban have arisen from the dead. So the soldiers don't have time to help us any more.

With them gone, Khalaa Gul is in a foul mood. I guess there's no one to flirt with. She snaps at everyone who gets in her way, and then one day she brings a new foreigner to take a look at us.

I'm mopping the floor of the kitchen and this lady walks in with her high heels, speaking that strange language.

She is a visitor from America. White and tiny and pretty, she has rosy cheeks and the bluest eyes I've ever seen. Her lips are painted pink and for some reason she's wearing a porani on her head, much like Khalaa Gul, where her hair shows through all over the place. Why do they bother?

While they look at me on my hands and knees with a dirty wet rag in my hands, Khalaa Gul says something to the lady. I catch their word for father. She's telling her about Baba. The lady nods. Then Khalaa Gul steps up and grabs my chin, lifting it up so she can see the scar.

I'm used to this by now. I guess it's the price of having it fixed.

A look of pity crosses the pretty lady's face. I think I can even see some tears in her eyes. After they leave and I've finally finished all my chores, I go back to my room and curl up in a corner with my porani wrapped around me, like I used to do.

Soraya comes in and walks right by me without seeing me at first. I must look like a bundle of laundry.

Then she comes back, takes a closer look at me and says, "Jameela?"

I've been peeking at her through my porani, but now I raise my head.

She bends her head closer.

"Are you all right?"

I wish there was some kind of surgery to mend me inside. There's a hole in me much bigger than the gap in my lip. But I can't tell Soraya that.

"What's wrong?" she says.

"I was just thinking of my father."

She sits down on my bed, her hands going limp in her lap.

"Forget about him."

"Do you think it was my lip that made him leave me?"

"Stop it," she says. "There's nothing you could have done. And you're not the only one to be left by your father." She looks down for a moment. "Men will leave their kids even when there's nothing wrong with them. And then sometimes, before they can come back to get them, they die." She sighs. "What do you think of this new donor lady?"

I shrug. "She seems all right."

"They all do when they first arrive."

"What about the soldiers? They didn't do anything wrong."

134

Soraya scowls. "They're invaders. They want to control us. They won't be happy until they change us so we're just like them."

"They fixed things. You should be grateful."

Soraya stands up and paces around our small room.

"I'm tired of being grateful."

I know what she means. I should be happy, and I am, but part of me still feels… I don't know. Empty?

I shouldn't feel this way. Isn't my life better? Subhanallah, I never thought I'd even be able to read. But there's still this hollow part of me that only family could fill.

Soraya walks back and forth in our small room, her hands on her waist, pulling the fabric of her dress tight. Her body has really developed in places. She paces a few more times. It feels like she's about to say something important so I wait quietly.

Finally she mutters, "I want a place of my own. Maybe I can get married."

She's never told me anything about herself.

"How long have you been here?"

"None of your business!"

I yell right back at her. "Then why are you bringing it up?"

I smile. Soraya grins at me. "Come. I can use some help in the kitchen."

I get to my feet and we pad down the hallway. When we arrive in the kitchen, Khalaa Gul and that new visitor are still there.

Khalaa Gul sees Soraya and says in a sickly sweet voice,

135

"There you are, Soraya, my dear. Could you do the biggest favor and make us a cup of tea?"

Soraya glances from Khalaa Gul to the visitor and nods. When she turns her back to them she looks at me and rolls her eyes.

Blue flames lick the black claw-like things on top of the stove where Soraya's boiling the tea.

When the disbelievers threw Prophet Abraham (peace be upon him) into the fire, he put his faith in God, saying, Hasbiyallahu wa ni'mal wakeel. God is enough for me and He is the best disposer of affairs. And God made the fire cool so it wouldn't burn him.

And when the Prophet Muhammad (peace be upon him) was betrayed by the hypocrites and the enemy gathered against them in huge numbers, the believers said Hasbiyallahu wa ni'mal wakeel.

Soraya takes the tea into Khalaa Gul and that new lady. Then she comes back and pours a cup for each of us. It's hot and milky and sweet, just the way I like it.

I smile at my friend and carefully take the first sip.

Hasbiyallahu wa ni'mal wakeel.

16

I THINK Khalaa Gul finally trusts us. Sometimes she sends Soraya and me to the marketplace to get things for the cook.

Khalaa Kareema gave me a gift of a new chadri. It's the light blue cotton kind with the mesh screen across the eyes. It leaves my hands free to carry things underneath.

I could dress like Soraya, just with loose clothes and a porani tied properly to cover my hair. Nothing wrong with that, but this is the way the wives of the Prophet (peace be upon him) dressed. And this is the way Mor would have dressed.

They were so strong. They were able to control their vanity. I want to be like them. And it's a lot easier than constantly holding my porani across my face like I did before.

When we go out I feel so mysterious. Men nod at me and step out of my way. There's nothing for them to see. Even those men with a disease in their hearts can't imagine disgusting things about me.

I thought I'd never get a feel for the streets of Kabul, but after a while, corners look familiar. Soraya is good at navigating. With her along, I don't have to worry about getting lost.

Today we take a different route, making our way onto a street that looks familiar to me.

I know where we are!

"We have to go to this man's shop!"

"Why?"

"This was the man who found me and brought me to the orphanage."

I see the place where I sat for all those hours. It's empty. Just some stains on the wall where someone threw their tea. There's the greasy mechanic shop. The place looks even smaller than I remember.

Agha Akram's shop is dark when we arrive. There's a new sticky strip with only a few fly carcasses stuck to it, hanging from the ceiling.

Soraya steps up looking at the meat hanging on hooks.

"We need to buy some bones. We might as well get them here."

I barely hear her. I'm listening for him.

Finally the back door opens and he walks in. He sees me and smiles, but he doesn't recognize me. How could he? I'm all covered up. He thinks we're just ordinary customers.

He comes toward us, pointing at the cuts of meat.

"What can I get you today?"

"Agha Akram. Assalaamu alaikum. Don't you remember me?"

He peers at me closely and shakes his head.

"I'm sorry, sister."

"It's me, Jameela."

138

He looks puzzled for a moment, and then his face lights up.

"Jameela! You were sitting outside my shop!"

"That's me and this is my friend Soraya, from the orphanage."

His face clouds over at the mention of the orphanage.

"And how have you managed there?"

"Subhanallah! Very well. I'm so glad you took me there!"

"You are?"

It is so wonderful to catch up! I ask about Tahira and the boys, and I ask about Khalaa without feeling the least bit of sadness. I still would have liked to stay with them, but I would have felt bad being a burden, and there's no doubt I would have been a burden.

Soraya looks bored. I'm sure this meeting isn't as fascinating for her as it is for me.

Finally I say, "Agha, it was so nice meeting you. Give my salams to Khalaa and Tahira."

But Agha Akram looks alarmed.

"No, no. You two must be our guests tonight. Your khalaa would never forgive me if I didn't bring you home to visit."

Soraya says, "It's getting late, Agha. We promised to be back soon. We do need some bones for the cook. How much?"

Agha Akram's face brightens.

"No, no. I won't take your money. Here. I'll get you some of the nicest bones."

He keeps insisting, so in the end we have no choice but to visit.

Soraya whispers to me, "We're going to be late. Khalaa Gul is going to have a fit."

I whisper back, "We won't stay long."

I don't remember it being such a short walk. Just a few side streets and we're there. I do remember the staircase being this dim and narrow.

When we arrive it's such a scene of joy. The little boys are bigger, but Tahira's the same. Khalaa is very gracious. She feeds us till we're ready to burst. Leaving is hard.

They say we must come back to visit and make us promise.

Agha Akram says he'll walk us. He brings along Tahira. I'm glad they're coming. It's past Maghrib time. It will be totally dark by the time we get back.

The streets are still bustling, mostly men doing the shopping for their wives. It looks so different in the dark.

Agha Akram leads us up one street and down another. After the third turn I wonder if he isn't supposed to go left at this junction. Instead he goes right and he seems so sure of himself that I don't correct him. Now we are in a completely unfamiliar part of town.

There's more damage here. Many of the houses have yet to be rebuilt from the years of war. There are fewer people on the streets.

Soraya whispers, "This doesn't look right."

Tahira says, "Baba, we're lost."

"Nonsense. This is a short cut. When we get to the end of that street down there we'll reach the main boulevard. You'll see."

140

He sounds sure of himself so we continue along, but the street he's talking about turns out to be a dead end.

I say, "Maybe we should knock on one of the houses and ask if they know how to get back to the main street."

Agha Akram snorts. "It's just a little farther. That was the wrong street. It's the one up ahead." But when we get to it, he turns to us looking confused. "I was sure it was this one."

I catch my breath. Something moves in the shadows, a little piece of blackness darker than the background.

It's a cat.

The cat looks very familiar. I'm sure I've seen that torn ear and those green eyes.

I start walking down another alley.

Agha Akram says, "Where are you going?"

"I think it's down here."

Tahira says, "It's so dark."

Soraya's right beside me. "This can't be the way."

But I'm sure it is.

At the end of the alley there's a large new door. But this is definitely the place. Before I can stop myself, I knock. Agha Akram looks surprised at my boldness.

Masood opens the door. He looks different, less scruffy. It takes me a moment to realize it's because he doesn't have the crutches any more.

"Come right in," he says. "My mother will see you in a moment." I examine his feet to see which one is artificial, but he's wearing socks with his sandals and it's hard to tell. But the way he walks, he seems to drag his right just a bit. I can't remember which foot was gone.

The courtyard has been cleared of bricks and rubble. They must have been working hard. It seems Baba has even started rebuilding with the undamaged bricks.

Masood looks back to see if we're following. He doesn't recognize me. How could he? It's such a feeling of power to be hidden away from view, to see him and know who he is while he has no clue. I do plan to tell him. Just not yet.

Soraya whispers, "Khalaa Gul will be going crazy wondering where we are."

"This won't take long."

Everything looks strange and smaller than I remember it. The furniture in the main room is more scratched and tattered, the walls dingier, the floors rough and uneven.

Did I really spend so many months here? It didn't look this shabby back then, but maybe that's because she doesn't have me to clean it any more.

I can't stop looking at Masood, and it seems he can't stop looking at Soraya. When he swallows, the knob in his throat bobs up and down.

"Please sit down," he says. "My mother will be here in a moment."

Agha Akram looks even more confused. Soraya is looking around at the surroundings, glancing at me like she's wondering what I'm up to. It's hard to tell what Tahira thinks. She's wrapped up like I am.

My heart is racing. I take deep breaths to calm it down. I can hear that woman talking to Masood in the kitchen, something about rents and tenants.

Agha Akram says, "They think we're here to rent the place."

A new curtain of beads separates the kitchen from the main room. She pushes it aside with a tinkling kind of noise and comes in. Her porani is still hanging half off her head, draped across her chest, not hiding the fact that her dress is too tight, especially across her breasts. The lines at the corners of her mouth are more etched, like she's been frowning a lot. Somehow that makes me happy.

She sees us and puts on a smile.

"Welcome! We've been expecting you. I'm sorry to take so long to receive you. I let my servant go for the day."

She doesn't have a servant.

Agha Akram speaks up. "I'm terribly sorry but there seems to be some kind of mistake."

"No, no. No mistake! I'm sure you'll find the room very comfortable for your," she glances at me, "wife and daughters. We should have the building finished in a month's time. Then you can move in."

Agha Akram tries to say something but she rides right over him.

"I know my husband should be speaking to you about this." She calls Masood. "Dear, go and get your *father*." She smiles apologetically at us.

Masood looks like he's going to argue, but then he ducks back behind that curtain of beads. In the silence, the tinkling of the beads is very loud.

Her face is red and there seems to be a film of sweat on her upper lip. She jumps up.

"Would you like to see the room?"

Agha Akram stands up.

"I'm sorry, sister, but we're not here to see any room. Myself and my daughter were just walking these young girls home when we got lost. We only wanted directions."

With narrowed eyes, she cocks her head and gets a sly look on her face.

"Walking these girls home?"

The way she says it makes me squirm. Agha Akram's face grows red. Soraya looks like she's going to slap her. Behind the mesh of Tahira's chadri, her eyes are wide.

Just then there's a loud banging at the door and she jumps to her feet.

To us she says, "Just wait here. I'll deal with you later."

And she runs to the door.

Agha Akram gets to his feet and says, "Come, let's go."

I say, "Please, Agha. In a minute. I want to see my father."

Agha Akram and Soraya look shocked. Masood comes back in, without Baba. He glances at us, then walks through to his mother in the courtyard talking to the new people.

It's not hard to overhear him say, "He won't get up."

She hisses, "Make him get up!" For a tiny moment I almost feel sorry for her. Then she goes back to the new people and in a loud voice says, "Well, brother, would you like to see the room now? I must warn you, there are other people here, too, so you need to make a decision soon."

Agha Akram whispers to me, "Jameela, we really can't stay much longer. We need to get home. Tahira has school tomorrow."

I'm being inconsiderate. We really should go. What difference will it make to see him?

Masood comes back into the salon, looking shy.

"My mother told me to help you."

Agha Akram stands up.

"Yes, please, can you let us know the way to the main boulevard? That's all we want. I need to take these girls back to the orphanage."

Masood hesitates, glancing at Soraya. She glances back at him and then looks down, her eyelashes sweeping against the curve of her cheeks. I think she's doing it on purpose. Masood gulps again.

"Let me show you the way."

He leaves his mother and guides us down several dark alleyways and corridors until finally we get to a gate that opens out on to the main street. Agha Akram is so relieved.

"Tashakur very much, young man."

Masood keeps staring at Soraya. She looks so modest with the way her porani frames her face.

He says, "So you stay at the orphanage?"

Soraya nods.

"It was nice meeting you."

Soraya nods again. I've never seen her so quiet.

At the orphanage, Khalaa Gul is waiting. When she sees us her jaw falls open. She looks ready to yell, but then she sees Agha Akram and Tahira.

Agha Akram says, "I'm so sorry, sister. I hope you remember me. I was the one who brought Jameela here. We met today and I insisted they come to dinner. This is my daughter. I'm so sorry to have kept them so late. We got lost on the way back."

Khalaa Gul puts on a smile.

"Oh, please don't worry about it, sir." Then she puts an arm around each of our shoulders and says much too cheerfully, "All is well."

Agha Akram frowns, says salams and leaves. As soon as he turns the corner, Khalaa Gul screams at us for being so late.

Soraya interrupts, "We're sorry about that. We really did get lost. Agha Akram gave us the bones for free. Here's the money back."

That makes her quiet. She counts the Afghanis in her hand, then she looks satisfied.

"Very well. Take these down to the cook. She'll have to use them tomorrow. It's too late today. Don't you ever try something like that again or I won't send you out. I'll go myself."

We both apologize again and are finally dismissed.

Down the hall, past the boys' section, I feel all jumbled up inside. How I wish I'd seen Baba! I can't help it. To have been so close… It makes me ache inside.

We burst into our room.

"Did you see your stepmother's dress?!" Soraya says. "I swear her breasts were going to pop right out! How can she wear things like that?"

"It's the fashion these days. I've seen worse!"

"It's all the foreigners. They're trying to be just like them. It's like that hadith. If the foreigners were to jump into a hole, they'd follow right behind them."

I can't laugh about that. Soraya tries to catch my eye.

"What's wrong, Jameela?"

"My father's one of them."

She's quiet for a moment. Finally she says, "Nothing you can do about that. It's too bad you didn't at least get to see him."

It hurts inside. I do miss him. And I wish he was like Agha Akram, there to take care of me. I wish I was Tahira.

Tahira's so lucky. No, not luck. There's no such thing. It's all qadr of Allah. She's blessed. She doesn't have a hole in her, a piece missing, like I do.

Soraya gets up and fiddles with the blanket on her bed, smoothing it even though it's already neat and tidy.

Quietly she says, "So was that your stepbrother who let us in?"

The longer I stare at her, the redder her face gets.

Finally she throws her pillow at me.

"Stop it!"

I smile.

That night, after we've prayed and got ready for bed, Soraya whispers into the darkness, "I thought you said your stepbrother was crippled."

"He must have got one of those artificial legs." She's silent for a while.

Something makes me say, "He's pretty good. You could do worse. But you would have to deal with *her*."

Soraya turns over on her bed, making the whole bunk shake.

"Oh, I can handle her." She adds, "Insha Allah."

17

A WEEK hasn't passed before Soraya comes bursting through the door of our classroom. She looks at me like she's itching to say something.

Holding the chalk pressed against the board, Khalaa Kareema frowns. All the students, including Arwa, turn to stare.

Soraya pulls me over to the side.

"She's here!"

"Who?"

"Her! Your stepmother." Soraya grabs my arm. Her hands are icy cold. "She wants to speak to me. What am I going to do?"

Khalaa Kareema puts the chalk down and comes over to us.

"What's the problem here? Jameela, your students are waiting."

Soraya grips my arm. "Come with me. I can't see her alone!"

I tell Khalaa Kareema what's happening.

She nods and says, "Fine, then. Go with your friend."

Soraya fixes her porani and adjusts her dress so it's as neat as possible.

"Do I look all right?"

I smile. "You look lovely." Then I pull my chadri over my head so it settles around my feet. I grab her arm and together we head toward the orphanage office.

Khalaa Gul is standing outside. She pulls me aside and says, "I want you to behave yourself. Don't ruin Soraya's chances. They look like a good family."

How could she even think I'd do such a thing?

Khalaa Gul and Agha Abdul Hakeem from the boys' side of the orphanage enter the room with us. They'll act as guardians for Soraya.

I have to admit, *she* is dressed quite modestly. Her dress isn't cut low this time and her porani is wrapped properly around her head and drapes across her chest even if it is flimsy and see through.

When she looks at Soraya, she smiles with her mouth but it doesn't reach her eyes.

She says, "I have come on behalf of my son. He is of marriageable age and he is looking for a wife."

It's Soraya's turn to respond. Elegantly she nods. She looks sweet. Like a pearl. I'm so proud of her.

My stepmother continues, "We're looking for a virtuous girl. One who isn't afraid of hard work. Who will fit into the family well."

Khalaa Gul pats Soraya on the shoulder.

"You couldn't have picked a finer one. Soraya's one of our best. I'll vouch for that."

149

Soraya's face turns pink at the praise, and she looks down at the floor. My stepmother nods.

After that they talk about everyday stuff, even the weather. At the end of it, she stands up and says her salams and leaves.

Khalaa Gul takes us aside.

"I'll do some checking on them, but it seems to me that everything will be fine." Then she dismisses us.

Soraya's spirits are soaring.

"I think that went well." She goes on and on about the short conversation, analyzing everything my stepmother said and everything she replied until I want to shut my ears.

"Which of his legs was artificial?" she says.

"I can't remember. You know she's going to work you hard."

Soraya nods. "I know, but then I work hard here, too. It's not going to be so bad. And it's not like she can make him leave me. I'll make sure of that."

I laugh. Maybe she will be able to handle her. It's possible. At least Masood would be good for her.

"Do you think I should have found a way at the house to tell Masood who I am?" I say.

Soraya frowns. "I'm not sure. Maybe not right now. Is that so awful?" She looks at me like she's asking permission. "Of course," she says. "I'll tell him. Later."

It only takes two more weeks of visits for my stepmother to make up her mind. I keep expecting Baba to show up for the meetings but he never comes. Khalaa Gul keeps asking about him, but my stepmother makes excuses. The second time she said he wasn't feeling well. This time he was away on business.

Soraya is so happy. Her face glows. Mor used to talk about noor, this kind of glow that a bride and groom get when they're righteous and about to get married. I always thought it was a myth, but here I see it myself.

Some of the other girls like Fyma and Raisa grumble. They're jealous. I wonder if I am, too. But I don't think it's jealousy that I'm feeling. I wouldn't want to marry Masood. Islamically I could. He isn't any relation to me. But I do feel strange about it.

She'll have a family again. My family.

It's that rip in me. I still feel it.

They've set the date, and the mehr. In two weeks' time we'll have the nikah right here in the orphanage. Agha Abdul Hakeem will act as Soraya's mehrem. The mehr is some jewelry. They haven't shown it to Soraya yet. She can't expect a lot. I can't help wondering if they bought it with the money from Mor's things, the money my father gave that woman for her mehr.

I know I shouldn't think like that. It does no good at all.

I hope Agha Akram wouldn't think this is a waste of the money he gave me from that mechanic. I want Soraya to have a new suit.

I ask Khalaa Gul and she lets us go shopping although we still need to pick up some things for the cook and her. We find some beautiful red material with some intricate embroidery on it. It shimmers and flows, and the color

151

looks fantastic against Soraya's skin. We get time to work on it. Soraya doesn't have to go to classes now. And Khalaa Kareema gives me time off so that I can help her.

With each stitch, I think of Mor, the last time we sewed together. She was making me Eid clothes with a new blue porani, showing me how to cut the fabric and sew the stitches, how to shape the shoulder so it would leave enough room for movement. She said to make the stitches tiny so they wouldn't come out, and with each stitch make a dua for Allah to protect the wearer so that even in the sewing there is worship.

Mor is gone and now Soraya will leave. I think of how empty this place will be.

I'm working on the neckline when I feel someone watching me. There's a flash of movement behind the doorway. Soraya picks her way through the pins and threads on the floor and peeks around the doorway. She grabs Arwa by the arm and drags her in.

"What's the matter?" says Soraya.

Arwa shakes her head, rubbing her dirty little face into Soraya's dress. Somehow Soraya doesn't mind. She pats Arwa's matted hair and even picks her up and carries her to my bunk. She sets her down on her lap and just holds her.

"It's going to be all right, insha Allah, you'll see."

Arwa's voice is muffled. She still has her face pressed to Soraya's chest.

"But you're the only one who's nice to me. And you're going."

Soraya glances at me. I feel like she's asking me to take over for her.

I look away. I know I shouldn't be like this. How can Soraya stand her? She's so filthy. If she'd just keep her face clean.

Soraya says, "You and Jameela can visit me. And I'll come to visit, too."

Arwa pulls away and looks up at Soraya.

"Really?"

"Yes. But right now Jameela and I have work to do."

Arwa glances at the material.

"Can I help?"

I groan. She'll be touching everything with her sticky hands.

Maybe Soraya's thinking that, too, because she frowns for a moment.

"This is too big for you to do."

"I could pick up all the scraps and put them in a pile. You want me to get the threads, too?"

"All right."

I want to groan again.

When Arwa has picked up every scrap and every thread, Soraya finally sends her on her way.

I've been wondering for a long time, so I finally ask.

"Soraya, why are you so close to her? She's so filthy."

"She came here when she was just a baby. Nobody knows who brought her. I always took care of her. I guess she could use some cleaning up."

"Some?"

Soraya frowns. "She's not that bad. I guess I don't notice it that much. I do tell her. She's just not very coordinated when it comes to washing."

"You're spoiling her."

Soraya doesn't say anything.

"It's a cruel world. She'll have to face that sooner or later."

Soraya still doesn't say anything.

"You're too soft on her!"

She sighs. "Someone has to be."

18

"ARWA, come with me."

She doesn't look up. "But I'm making my gift for Soraya."

I look closer. She's twisting some of the scrap material she picked up, tying it with some of the thread.

"What is that?"

"It's a ribbon for Soraya's hair." Arwa's face is smudged. A little stream runs out from her left nostril, and she's licking at it with her tongue. It makes me feel sick, but it's too late. She's coming over already.

"Where are we going?"

If I tell her she might run away, so I just say, "You'll see."

As we get closer to the bathroom she slows her steps. There's growing alarm on her face.

I grab her hand before she can turn and bolt. She's pulling back. I have to drag her, trying not to lose my temper.

"Don't you want to be clean for the wedding? Think how happy Soraya will be."

That does the trick. She stops hanging back.

155

I hope the water's not cold by now. I warmed it up myself, two batches. One for Soraya and one for Arwa. I already had my bath. I don't mind it cold.

Arwa touches the water in the steaming bucket.

"It's warm."

And then suddenly she strips off all her clothes, dumping them on the ground.

I say, "Yooo! You're not supposed to do that."

She looks up at me completely unashamed.

"Do what?"

I cover my face so I don't see her private parts.

"Put your pants back on! You're not supposed to show anyone between your bellybutton and your knees. That's private. Actually, I'll turn around, and you wash that part first. Scrub it real good and then put your pants back on."

She reaches for the precious bit of soap in my hand but I pull it away. Soap costs money. I can't stand the thought of it touching her private parts.

"Wet your hands. Then I'll let you rub them on the soap."

Khalaa Kareema gave me this soap. I feel kind of greedy about it. I already let Soraya use it for her bath and it's almost gone.

"Like this," I say, showing her how to lather it. When she finishes that area, I can look again. I tell her to scrub her face. She's too gentle. I make her scrub harder, particularly around the nose.

"But I'll get suds up it."

"They won't hurt you. Come on, now your hair."

156

That's much harder so I help her. When she scoops out the water to rinse I see her rib bones like the fingers of a hand clasped around her back and sides. Subhanallah, she's so tiny and vulnerable. If I wanted I could do anything to her. She's lucky she can trust me.

She flips her sopping wet hair to the side and squints up at me.

"Done?" There are still suds in the top part.

"Not yet." I bend down and rinse them away. Then I show her how to scrub the rest of her and make wudu. She doesn't even know how to make wudu!

Cleaned up, she looks a lot better. She'll never be beautiful but she's all right. I turn my back as she gets dressed. And then I take out a comb and work through her hair.

While I'm braiding it I have a strange feeling. Mor used to braid mine just like this, with her right leg tucked up under her, sitting on the charpaee, with an elastic band clenched in her teeth.

I grab her hand. She doesn't flinch this time, and I look her right in the eye.

"If I warm up the water for you, will you take more baths?"

She looks down at the floor and nods, but I tell her to look me in the eye and answer out loud. I want to hear her promise.

"Okay. I will."

"Good," I say, picking up my blue porani. The end is ragged where I ripped off a piece to tie around that marker for Mor's grave.

I notch another bit and rip off a strip. I tuck it into Arwa's sleeve.

"Now, use this cloth to wipe your nose. I never want to see it running again."

"What do I do when it gets dirty?"

I take a deep breath so I don't snap at her.

"You will wash it and spread it out to dry. Every night before you go to sleep if you have to."

"Can I use some of your soap?"

I don't have much, but I nod anyway.

"Here." I break off a piece and hand it to her.

"Tashakur, Jameela!" And she hugs me. For once I don't mind.

I tell Arwa to go out so I can change into my nice clothes. On top of it I put my blue chadri. No one can see how I look underneath, but at least I know I look nice.

When we're ready we go down to the office where Soraya and Zeba are holed up in a room on the side. I knock on the door and Zeba lets us in.

Soraya looks as beautiful as a red rose. Zeba did her hair up in a bun with bits dangling down the sides like I've seen on posters of Bollywood movie stars. Where did she get the makeup? Her lips match the dress.

I leave my chadri on even though it's all women. It doesn't feel very private here.

Soraya's face lights up when Arwa dangles her "gift" before her. I can't believe she tells Zeba to pin it into her hair. It dangles in front of her bun like a red hairy caterpillar.

Khalaa Gul slips in without knocking. She looks at Soraya and smiles.

"How much more time do you need?" Then she picks up the bag that's beside Zeba and hunts through the plastic jars and bottles. She takes out this black tube and unscrews it. It has the tiniest black brush. Khalaa Gul starts brushing Soraya's eyelashes with it.

"This will make them stand out."

But her eyelashes already stand out. She's got the longest, prettiest lashes I've ever seen.

When Khalaa Gul has finished, Soraya's eyelashes have little black clumps along them and they look like they're made of plastic.

I think the noor is gone. I can hardly see it under all that makeup. But it's none of my business, so I keep my mouth shut.

We pin the red porani that came with the material to her hair. It does a lot to hide Arwa's ribbon.

Soraya will stay in this room. That way she won't have to cover up in front of the men, only when they come to ask her permission.

The door opens again and my stepmother comes in. I'm so glad I have my chadri on, but even then I'm shaking inside, praying that Allah gives Soraya strength to deal with her.

The woman is back to wearing the tight revealing clothes: peacock blue with splotches of embroidery on it, and she has more makeup on than Soraya.

She has a little jewelry case in her hands.

159

"This is the mehr," she says, and takes out a tiny little gold set complete with earrings, necklace, bracelets and ring. Elegantly, Soraya tilts her head to each side so she can put the earrings on and then bends forward so she can fasten the clasp of the necklace. It almost looks like she's bowing to her!

The ring is a bit tight. She tries to put it on Soraya's finger but it won't go, so Soraya does it herself. The bracelets are tight, too.

My stepmother smiles and nods and goes back outside to join the men.

Something makes me follow her. I can't seem to stop myself. And when I see him there, I know why I had to come in here.

A fist has grabbed my heart. It's holding tight and won't let go.

He has his face turned away from me, talking to Agha Abdul Hakeem, nodding and laughing. His hair is long and wavy, and his beard is gone. He looks like one of those Bollywood movie stars. He's got that same puffy soft look to him.

He's joking with the orphanage manager and then laughing at his own joke. How can he be laughing?

I don't know what I was expecting. That he would be drunk or dazed with opium? Not this. He's still laughing and he turns to look around the room and sees me standing in the doorway. He stops laughing for a moment, then turns back to tell another joke.

He can't recognize me. I'm wearing the chadri.

She goes over and whispers in his ear. He listens so attentively. So respectfully. He wasn't that respectful with Mor.

Doesn't anyone ever ask about me? Doesn't anyone ever wonder where I went? What do they tell people? Her sister saw me. She knew I existed. What did they tell her when I was gone?

I turn around and go back into Soraya's room. She looks so pretty. When I see her I feel only happiness for her. But now I do feel a twinge, not of jealousy but of yearning. I would like to get married one day, too. I wonder what her first night with Masood will be like, and then I blush and feel ashamed to be thinking of such things. She looks so happy. And I realize I'm smiling. Zeba is glued to her side. Khalaa Gul is standing nearby, perched on her high heels.

Arwa is running around annoying people. As she runs past, I grab her arm and shove her into a corner.

"Sit down!" I feel a bit sorry when I see her lip quiver, but she has to learn.

Soraya sees me and calls me over to her other side. She locks her arm through mine and clasps my hand. It makes me feel good.

"I'm so nervous!" she whispers.

She doesn't look nervous, just excited. I hope Masood stands up for her better than he stood up for me. But then things might be different for Soraya. She's so strong. I was so weak back then. I can't believe how I cowered and cringed all the time.

That woman comes to the door and then walks right up

in front of me, obviously expecting to take my place beside Soraya. Soraya grips my hand more tightly, but I pull myself away and get up quickly.

"They're about to begin," she says.

We all settle down. I'm in a corner with Arwa.

In the next room, the mullaa starts with a khutba in Arabic, and then in Farsi he starts talking about the duties of a husband to his wife. I can understand almost all of it. With all the Farsi girls in the orphanage I've picked up a lot. Then in Pushto he talks more about the wife's and the husband's rights toward each other. And he talks about kindness and mercy to all family members.

I watch *her* during all this talk. She's chewing her lip. I wonder if she's even listening. I wonder if her conscience bothers her. What did she tell herself that made it okay to make Baba get rid of me?

Then we can hear the mullaa getting to his feet with the other men. I take out my good porani and put it over the flimsy one that's covering Soraya's hair, so she's properly covered when the men come in to get her permission. She's still got all that makeup on, but she looks very modest. The mullaa and Baba and one other witness stand outside the doorway until *she* says it's all right for them to enter.

My breath catches in my throat when I see Baba again. He looks quite dignified in his kurtha and salwar. I recognize it. It's one of her old husband's fancy outfits.

They stand before Soraya. This is her moment. Three times they ask if she agrees to marry Masood. Three times she blushes and whispers, "Yes."

162

Baba steps forward then. With a dramatic flourish, he pats Soraya on her head and says, "You will be like my own daughter to me!"

I gasp so loudly that everyone turns and looks. I wish I could run out of this room. Or I wish the floor could open up and swallow me. They keep staring at me.

It takes forever for them to look away. The mullaa is all sympathy. He touches Baba on the arm and says, "May this girl be a comfort in your loss."

Around the room many say, "Ameen."

That woman turns to Soraya and whispers loudly enough for everyone to hear, "His daughter was lost." She pauses. "In a minefield."

This time I don't gasp, but Soraya does.

Khalaa Gul nods sympathetically. From across the room Soraya's eyes meet mine. Her mouth is open. She looks like she doesn't know what to do.

The best thing about a chadri is that unless you make a sound, nobody can tell that you're crying.

The ceremony goes on. That woman puts her arm around Soraya's shoulders.

Am I the only one who sees her glance at the people watching to make sure her affection looks genuine?

And Baba, bending down to kiss Soraya on the forehead, welcoming her to the family, to my family. When was the last time he kissed me like that? I can't even remember.

Soraya's jaw is set in a grim line. Her excitement is gone.

And then the men go back and offer Soraya's hand in marriage to Masood. We can hear him accept.

That woman looks happy. She pulls out a bag filled with rose petals and marigolds. Red and orange petals cling to Soraya's cheeks and plastic eyelashes. They must tickle.

She's smiling now. The sweet fragrance of roses mixes with the spicy scent of marigolds and spreads around the room.

Baba passes a tray of fancy sweets. There are sugar-coated almonds, sticky orange gelabis, and cubes of pink and green sheer payra. These are some of the most expensive sweets you can buy.

Khalaa Gul looks impressed. She takes several pieces.

They might as well be made of sawdust. I can't eat them.

Too soon, it's time for Soraya to leave. Khalaa Gul bawls so loudly I'm sure the men can hear. Soraya sees me across the room and raises her eyebrows. I have to smile. And smiling feels so strange.

Soraya picks up Arwa and says, "I didn't recognize you! You're so clean!" Arwa giggles and hugs her around the neck so hard Soraya's Bollywood hair is getting mussed up.

Next comes Zeba. Soraya hugs her for such a long time, I feel a prick of jealousy. I wonder what she's whispering to her. They glance at me a couple of times, and Zeba nods.

Finally Soraya gives Zeba one last hug and lets her go.

Now it's my turn to say goodbye and I can't. I just stare at her through the mesh of the chadri.

She grabs me tight and whispers into my ear, "This isn't the end of it."

Through the blue fabric I whisper back, "No! Don't do anything to ruin your future."

164

Soraya hugs me a bit tighter.

"Don't worry. You'll see." She grabs both my hands and pulls back to see me better. "I'm going to miss you. Bring Zeba. Come visit me."

I just nod. My throat is too tight to say anything. And then she lets go, and she's gone. I can see the back of her, wearing my new porani, also my gift to her, with *her* walking by Soraya's side.

Hasbiyallahu wa ni'mal wakeel.

19

I'M WORKING with Arwa and some of the other girls on their math lesson when Khalaa Gul comes in with Zeba right behind her. Khalaa Gul speaks to Khalaa Kareema for a while in hushed tones. Khalaa Kareema seems upset.

I hear her say, "It's the middle of the class! Can't she wait half an hour?"

Khalaa Gul puts her hand on my shoulder and leads me into the hallway.

"Here's some money. Cook wants you to go to that same meat shop to see if you can get some more bones for free. Don't use the money unless you have to."

I can't believe her. She gets lots of money from all those foreigners. Agha Akram's family needs to eat, too.

She says, "And while you're out there, I need some eggplant and yogurt to take home with me. You can find a shop along the way. You're a bright girl. Take Zeba and don't be too long about it."

Now I'm doing her shopping, too?

We walk down many of the hallways until I realize Zeba's leading me outside.

"Wait! I have to get my chadri."

Zeba looks annoyed.

"Don't you get tired of wearing that thing? The Taliban are gone, you know."

I don't bother answering.

The streets are crowded. The sun is warm. Spring is on the way. I can smell it on the breeze. I'm almost glad I was sent on this errand.

Zeba's hair flows out behind her in waves, and her kameez is tight and cut low. The same men that lower their gaze and step aside for me to pass brush right up against her. She doesn't seem to realize it's not an accident.

It's been six days since Soraya left. I miss her.

Zeba says, "Did you see the way Fyma and Raisa have taken over? They were just waiting for their chance! The way they told Fazeela to move out of that corner of the prayer hall so they could sit down in her place. Who do they think they are? I'd like to tell them off."

"So why don't you?"

A dirty young boy bumps right into Zeba then. I can see him squeeze her breast. This time Zeba gets mad and slaps him on the head. He runs off laughing.

I know I shouldn't find it funny, but somehow I can't help smiling. The boy was so dirty and bold.

Zeba is watching me. I make sure no giggles escape. For a while we walk in silence. She adjusts her porani so that it covers her hair and chest a bit.

I wonder what's happening with Soraya. I keep thinking of how she said it wasn't over.

It isn't that hard now to find my way to Agha Akram's shop. He glances at Zeba and says, "Where's your pretty friend?"

Zeba glares at him.

His face goes red and he stammers a bit. I don't think he meant to insult her.

"I mean, that other girl, the one you came with before."

I tell him about Masood and his face clouds over. He glances at Zeba.

"You mean she married that boy we met that night? At that house? With that woman?"

I can tell he's wondering if Zeba knows the relationship between Masood and me. I'm so scared he's going to say something, but finally he just adds, "Subhanallah. How the qadr of Allah works!"

When it's time to pay for the bones Agha Akram keeps insisting he give them to us for free.

Finally I say, "Please, Agha. The orphanage receives donations. You should be paid."

Agha Akram finally nods and accepts the money, although not the full amount, I'm sure.

On the way out, Zeba says, "You could have just told Khalaa Gul you had to pay him and then kept the extra money. Then we could have got a kulfi or something."

What did Soraya ever see in this girl?

We pick up the eggplant and yogurt at a shop down the road. The way Zeba bargains is amazing. I can only stand there in admiration.

The man who owns the shop seems to be enjoying it, too. He's waving his arms around, telling her he has five children to feed and she's stealing food out of their mouths. Zeba yells right back, saying that this is for the orphanage and we have many more children to feed.

But this isn't for the orphanage. It's for Khalaa Gul.

It's amazing how easily Zeba can lie. Doesn't it bother her? He knocks the price down by an Afghani but still she argues. He goes to serve another customer.

I whisper to Zeba, "We're already getting it for a bargain. Let's just pay and go."

"Wait. He'll come down another bit. I'm sure of it."

It takes another ten minutes of haggling but sure enough he does lower the price even more. When he dishes the yogurt into a container and hands us the eggplants, he nods at Zeba with a smile on his face, and Zeba grins right back.

At the street, instead of going back to the orphanage, she turns left.

"But we've finished," I say.

"You don't want to go back without seeing Soraya, do you?" She plunges into an alleyway. "It's down this way."

"How do you know?"

"I went to visit her a few days ago, when Khalaa Gul sent me to the market."

"How did you find your way?"

Zeba shrugs. "Soraya told me."

"When?!"

"When she was hugging me at the nikah. She wanted

me to bring you today. That's why I told Khalaa Gul about getting the bones for free."

Zeba's walking so fast it's hard to keep up. We pass three alleyways, charge down this street past the curve and up that way.

After five minutes things start to look familiar.

"It's very noisy around here," Zeba grins. "Hear that? Sounds like someone's having an argument."

Slowly Zeba turns up toward that woman's house. Some of the doors to the other houses are open. Three old women have brought their stools out into the street and are sifting through grains of rice, their ears cocked in the direction of my stepmother's house. A man is in the lane, taking his time to adjust the chain on his bicycle. Other people are just standing around, barely disguising the fact that they're listening.

Now I can make out Masood's voice.

"Do you think I'm going to let you treat Soraya like you treated her?!"

The gate is wide open. Zeba pauses in front of it. I hang back.

Soraya is standing on the other side of Masood, away from *her*. My stepmother's hair looks messy. Her porani is off her head and sideways.

She glances at the gate and says, "Don't be silly…dear. I'd never treat your wife…badly." She gathers herself up to stand tall. "And I never treated her badly either, as Allah is my witness."

Soraya hisses like a cat. "How dare you bring Allah into

170

this to prop up your lies! Do you really think I don't know?"

My stepmother laughs nervously. Her tone goes soft.

"Come inside. Let's talk about this calmly."

Two of the old women glance at each other, their hands across their mouths to hide their smiles.

Soraya finally notices us standing there.

"Zeba!" She rushes forward and hugs her tightly.

Many emotions seem to pass over my stepmother's face, from annoyance to the realization that she has visitors who could take their own versions of what's happening farther out into the world.

She steps forward.

"Zeba! How nice to see you again! Daughter…dear, do invite your friend in. We'll make some tea."

Zeba turns and grabs my arm.

"Look who I brought!"

I hold my breath. She must not tell. Soraya looks worried, too.

Then Zeba says, loudly enough for everyone on the street to hear, "I brought Jameela."

20

THE THREE old women with the rice gasp, almost dropping their bowls. They jump up and peer at me. The man with the bicycle stares, too. And the other people who were just standing around send the children, perhaps to spread the news.

Zeba looks confused. Masood's lower jaw is hanging open. My stepmother's face is red and swollen. She looks like she's getting ready to say something but Baba comes running out of the house right toward me. He looks half wild, with his eyes bloodshot and his hair flying in all directions.

He grabs my arm and yells, "Where have you been?!"

The neighbors who are still hanging around cast sidelong glances at each other while he drags me in and slams the gate.

Masood is shaking his head. To Soraya he says, "If I don't leave now, I'll lose my job." He nods at me. "I'm glad you're not dead."

When he goes through the gate to leave I can see the

neighbors' kids peeking in. Baba bolts the door. When he turns around he doesn't look wild any more. His gaze shifts between his wife on one side and me, Soraya and Zeba on the other.

My stepmother finally finds her voice. She turns to Soraya.

"What is going on here? Is this your doing?"

Soraya shakes her head. "It's you who have done things."

Zeba still looks confused. She must think we're all crazy.

My stepmother starts saying, "As Allah is my witness..."

I interrupt. "Don't." With Masood gone and the door closed I can take off my chadri. She and Baba stare like they're seeing me for the first time.

Then I remember my lip. I can feel the scar where they stitched the open sides of it together.

Baba takes a step forward.

"My dear, I never thought I'd see the day you would be whole."

I clench my fists tightly to my sides so I don't strike him.

He touches my arm. "Come, let us sit down and talk this through."

I can't very well pull away. Not with Zeba watching. He leads me by the elbow through the courtyard, past the spot where that woman rubbed out my name in the dirt. We walk on all the floors I endlessly mopped and past all the cushions I beat the dust out of, and into the salon to sit on the tattered furniture.

Zeba nudges Soraya. "Please tell me what is happening."

173

I speak up. "He is my father, and this…is my stepmother."

It's like I can see the thoughts turning in Zeba's head. Everyone in the room knows Zeba has the power to disgrace our family even more. Does she remember the things Baba and that woman said about me at the nikah?

Is Zeba going to laugh? She's always looked for ways to put me down. I brace myself. But the look she sends my way is full of pity. Pity from Zeba! I'd rather she had laughed.

Baba glances at Zeba and turns to Soraya, "Please, dear, bring our guests some tea."

Etiquette demands that we refuse at least a few times. Zeba says that we need to get back to the orphanage. My father insists. Again we make an excuse to leave. Again he insists. This time Zeba glances at Soraya and says, "Maybe we can stay just for a little while. We don't want to impose."

That woman plants herself on the couch. Soraya leaves to make the tea. I wish I could go with her.

Baba sits down, too. His eyes aren't as red. More glassy.

He glances at Zeba, clears his throat and turns to me with a big fake smile.

"Daughter, dear, it is so good to see you! Were you really staying all that time at the orphanage?"

I nod.

"They must be taking very good care of you."

"Yes. They are."

Zeba says, "This is such a nice house. You are so lucky! You and Soraya will be sisters now!"

For a moment we're all frozen. Does she think I'm mov-

174

ing back here? Baba's lips are parted. My stepmother is watching him. Within the awkwardness of their silence, I have my answer. He doesn't need to say anything. I understand perfectly.

Zeba looks confused. She's about to speak, but something makes me interrupt.

"It would be...nice to live here, but really, I couldn't leave the orphanage! I've grown so fond of the children. Especially Arwa. With Soraya gone, she depends on me. I want to be a good role model for her, the way my mother was for me. May Allah have mercy on her soul."

They all have the decency to say, "Ameen."

We're quiet for a while. The only sound is the rattle of cups and saucers coming from the kitchen. In a moment Soraya comes in with the tea things.

Zeba says, "But wouldn't you want to stay here, with your family?"

Baba's squirming. *She's* looking at the floor like she might even be ashamed. I could make them look really bad if I wanted to.

"I couldn't leave Khalaa Kareema," I say.

Soraya turns to Baba and my stepmother.

"Khalaa Kareema is one of the teachers. She says Jameela is the best student she's ever had. She even thinks Jameela will be a teacher one day."

My stepmother has stopped staring at the floor. She's looking at me with pure hatred in her eyes.

Baba's staring at me like he's really seeing me for the first time.

Soraya continues, "I heard them talking. Khalaa Kareema said that they might even pay Jameela. I think around a hundred Afghanis a day."

Baba says, "That's half of what Masood makes!"

Zeba nods. "I heard them talking, too."

Baba's staring at me with a strange look on his face. Zeba runs her hand along the cushions of the sofa and sighs.

"I can't imagine why you wouldn't want to live here, but at least you can visit!"

My stepmother's face has gone red. She can't tell me not to visit. Not with Zeba here.

I take the cup of tea that Soraya hands me and say, "Oh, yes! I would love to visit! I would like that very much."

She's glaring at me. It feels so good.

The tea is thick with buffalo milk. My stepmother frowns. Maybe she's thinking of the extravagance. There's a bowl of sugar on the tray.

Something makes me take five heaping spoonfuls to stir into my tea.

21

I FEEL strange when it's time to leave, stepping through that gate. The ladies come to their doors to watch us pass, covering their mouths with their flimsy poranis and staring at me like they can't believe their eyes.

"Jameela, child? Is it really you?" says one of the old women.

I'm wearing my chadri so she can't tell. I nod. She shakes her head, glancing at my stepmother's house in disgust, and retreats back to her home.

I find myself getting excited when we get to the head of our street and I can see the orphanage. Nothing feels more like home. Not her house, not that first place, not even Agha Akram's.

Alhamdu lillah, this is where I belong. Allah's been very kind to me.

I don't stop Zeba when she sees Khalaa Gul in the office and blurts out where we've been and what she learned.

Khalaa Gul turns to me, astonished.

"Jameela! Why didn't you tell me?"

"My stepbrother is a good man. I didn't want to ruin it for Soraya."

Khalaa Gul is quiet. I wonder if she's replaying all the things they said during the nikah and the visits.

Finally I say, "Khalaa, I'm tired. Is it okay if I go lie down?"

Khalaa looks at me for a moment like she's forgotten I was here. Then she nods.

"Of course."

It doesn't take long for the news to spread all over the orphanage, even to the brothers' side. Somehow I manage to get through all the expressions of shock and concern.

The next day I'm back teaching the same math lesson when there's another knock on the door.

It's Khalaa Gul and she wants me to step into the hallway so we can talk in private.

She seems uncomfortable. She keeps opening her mouth, hesitating and then closing it again.

Finally she says, "You know, Jameela, we've become very fond of you here at the orphanage. Khalaa Kareema couldn't manage her class without you."

She couldn't have interrupted my class just to tell me this.

She clears her throat.

"I know we've never talked about money. We really don't have a lot, but one day I'm sure I could put something aside to pay you for some of what you do around here. It wouldn't be much, you understand."

I nod.

She clears her throat again.

"What I'm trying to tell you is that you'll always be welcome here. I know that if the parents of any of our girls come for them, I'm obliged to turn them over, but if it's really in the best interest of the girl to stay, then we can always find a way to work things out."

"Khalaa, could we talk about this later? I'm in the middle of a lesson right now."

Khalaa Gul frowns. "Well, no. I'm afraid we can't. You see, you've got a visitor."

What is she talking about?

"It's your father. I can't believe he has the nerve to show his face here after all that's happened!"

That woman kicked him out! She must have. He never would have left on his own.

"Where is he?"

"He's in the office. Before you see him, please do consider that you're welcome here, and I'll do whatever I can to make sure we can pay you...one day."

"All right. Can I see him?"

She hesitates for a moment, then nods. She can't very well refuse.

Baba looks like a tank ran over him. His clothes have dark stains all over them and a tear in the shoulder, his hair needs combing and his eyes are wild.

He jumps up when he sees me.

"Jameela! I've left her. That place wasn't good for us. That wicked woman! I never should have married her."

He glances at the other people in the office. Is he wondering if they believe him?

179

He takes me by the arm into the same small room we used for the nikah. He sits down on the corbacha and pulls me down to sit beside him.

"Take that thing off! I want to see your pretty face."

The door is closed, so I remove my chadri. He grabs hold of my hand again, massaging it in his own.

"Oh, my dear girl. To see you whole is more than I ever wished for. I never should have married that awful woman. She could twist any man to evil. But that's all behind us now. We'll find some new place, you and I, and we'll start a new life. Now that you can read and make some money teaching, we'll be fine. I always meant to send you to school. You do know that, don't you?"

He doesn't wait for me to answer. Quickly he adds, "And with your lip fixed, who says we won't find some rich man who'll pay a nice dower to have you."

His hands are shaking. He pats the breast pocket of his kurtha and I hear the sloshing of some liquid in a tiny bottle. Then he glances at me and moves his hand down to another pocket. He fumbles for a moment and manages to pull out a cigarette.

When did he start smoking? He tries to light a match but his hands are shaking too much.

I'm not going to light it for him.

He shoves the bent match and cigarette back into his pocket and turns to face me again.

"So what do you say, dear?"

"What do I say to what?"

"Come with me! We'll go somewhere they don't know us

180

and start a new life. I'll find you a nice husband. We'll be rich. Never mind that awful woman and her treacherous son. I promise I'll take good care of you!"

He just watches me for a moment, an impossible expression of hope on his face.

"Come on, daughter. It's getting late. We should be going if we want to make good time out of this God-forsaken place!"

Asthaghfirullah!

I take a deep breath.

"I hope you find a good place, Baba, but I can't go with you."

"Yes, you can! That witch, she knows she can't keep you. Not when your own father has come. We can leave right now. Nothing can stop us."

He starts to get up, but this time I'm the one who grasps his arm to stop him.

"No, Baba. I didn't say it right. It's not that I can't go with you. It's that I won't go with you. I'm staying here."

For a long time Baba just stares at me. The expression on his face gradually changes from shock to rage. Then he glances at the door.

That's right. He can't do anything to me. Not with all those people in the other room. But still, I should get out of his reach.

I get to my feet and put on my chadri.

"Assalaamu alaikum, Baba." Peace be upon you. And I mean it.

He doesn't reply. I'm glad he doesn't beg. My last

glimpse of him is sitting on the corbacha staring at his empty hands.

Whatever happens to him is not my responsibility. Men are supposed to be the caretakers of women, not the other way around. He's on his own.

Still, it isn't easy. I do wish him the best. And I do hope he is all right.

When I step through the doorway, Khalaa Gul grabs me around my neck.

"You're staying!"

Was she listening? I shouldn't be surprised.

"Yes, I'm staying."

She's so happy that she chatters on about class schedules and how she might find me my own classroom.

But one thing is still bothering me. I wasn't exactly truthful yesterday at their house, when I told them about Arwa.

When Arwa comes running up the hall to greet me, her face is clean, her clothes are clean and even her nose is clean. I don't hesitate to hug her.

I watch her so she makes wudu properly, and I don't even yell when she makes the same mistake three times. When I've tucked the last few strands of her hair in around her porani, and she's all ready for prayer, I give her a hug like she's the very best and I wouldn't exchange her for all the money in the world.

For a long time she hugs me back, really tightly for one so small. It feels strange.

Finally she lets go.

I pat her on her shoulder and say, "You know, Arwa. I'm going to tell you something my mother always told me. I want you to really pay attention and try to follow it."

Arwa's eyes are huge, the expression on her face solemn.

"What is it?" she whispers.

"If you can't be beautiful, you should at least be good. People will appreciate that."

She repeats the words to herself as she makes her way into the prayer hall.

Insha Allah, she'll be all right.

Author's Note

JAMEELA'S story is set shortly after the American invasion of Afghanistan in 2001. It is fiction, but it is based on a true incident.

Some years ago I read a report on children in crisis that was issued by Afghanistan's department of orphanages. Buried in the report was one paragraph that broke my heart. It was the story of a girl named Sameela. Her mother had died during the war, her father had remarried and the new stepmother didn't want her, so the father took her to the marketplace and left her there. She ended up living in one of the largest orphanages in Kabul.

There are no accurate statistics on the number of civilian and especially child casualties in Afghanistan due to the war.

When countries go to war, it is always civilians, especially children, who suffer the most.

Rukhsana Khan

Acknowledgments

I'D LIKE to acknowledge the help of Najibah and Karima Yousufi, who are from Kandahar and were kind enough to vet the manuscript for accuracy.

And many thanks to my sister-in-law Sarah Alli, who is from Kabul, for her insights into culture and everyday life.

Glossary

Afghani — The name of the currency in Afghanistan (the people are called Afghan).

Agha — Uncle in Pushto; a term of respect applied to any older male.

Alhamdu lillah — Arabic phrase meaning "all praise for God."

Allah — Muslim name for God.

Alaihi salam — Arabic phrase meaning "peace be on him."

Ameen — Said like "amen" after a prayer.

Assalaamu alaikum — Muslim greeting meaning "peace be upon you."

Asthaghfirullah — Arabic phrase meaning "God forgive me."

Baba — Pushto word for father.

Banjaan — Pushto word for eggplant; a Pushto dish containing eggplant, potatoes, onions, tomato sauce and yogurt.

Baraka — Literally means blessing. "Each child brings their own baraka" means that God provides for each child He creates.

Burka — Another word for chadri.

Chador — Literally a shawl, but can also refer to outer garments.

Chadri — Farsi name for a long veil that covers from head to below the knees, often with a mesh for the eyes to see through. Also called a burka.

Charpaee — A cot made of wood and jute string.

Chitral hat—A beret-like hat, flat on the top with a rolled-up cuff.

Corbacha — Long flat cushions placed on the floor and used instead of sofas.

Dhikr—A counting off of praise for God—33 times Subhanallah (glory be to God), 33 times Alhamdu lillah (all praise for God) and 33 times Allahu Akbar (God is great).

Dua—A small prayer.

Dusterkhan — A type of tablecloth laid on the ground to place food on.

Eid—An Arabic word meaning celebration. There are two Eid festivals in Islam—one after Ramadan, the month of fasting, and the other on the tenth day of Dhul Hijjah, the culmination of the pilgrimage in Mecca.

Fajr—Early morning prayer, from dawn until sunrise.

Fard—Obligatory prayers.

Farsi— The Persian language.

Gelabis—Sticky fried orange sweets.

Ghusl — The ritual bath that purifies one after a major impurity such as menstruation. Also performed on dead bodies before burial.

Hadith—Saying of the Prophet Muhammad (peace be upon him).

Hajj — The annual pilgrimage to Mecca that each Muslim is required to perform once in their lifetime, if they have the means.

Haram—Forbidden.

Hasbiyallahu wa ni'mal wakeel—Arabic phrase meaning "God is enough for me and He is the best disposer of affairs."

Hijab—The headscarf worn by Muslim women to cover their hair.

Imam — Leader of prayer (Arabic word that literally means "in front of").

Inna lillahi wa inna ilaihi rajioon — Arabic phrase spoken when someone dies, meaning "From God we come and to Him is our return."

Insha Allah — Arabic phrase meaning "If God wills."

Iqama — Second call to prayer (right before prayer is about to begin).

Isha — Last prayer of the day, prayed before bed, when night becomes fully dark until around midnight.

Jamat — Congregation.

Janaza — Muslim funeral prayer.

Jumaa — Literally Friday, the Muslim holy day of the week, when a special Jumaa or Friday prayer is said.

Kaaba — The most sacred shrine in Islam, situated in Mecca.

Kameez — Dress.

Khalaa — Aunt in Pushto; also a term of respect for any older female.

Khutba — A sermon given on Fridays and at weddings and Eid occasions.

Kofta — Meatball.

Kufi — Small hat.

Kulfi — A creamy frozen treat.

Kurtha — A tailored type of tunic.

Maghrib — Prayer performed right after sunset.

Medina — A city north of Mecca that contains the second most sacred site in Islam, the Prophet's Mosque (peace be upon him).

Mehr — The gift that a man gives to his bride on marriage.

Mehrem — A member of the opposite sex who is closely related and whom you cannot marry, i.e., father, brother, nephew, mother's brother, father's brother. They often act as chaperone.

Mor — Pushto word for mother.

Mullaa — Like a Muslim priest.

Naan — Flat bread.

Nafil — Extra "bonus" prayers one can perform.

Nikah — Wedding ceremony, where the bride offers her hand in marriage and the groom accepts by giving her a gift of the mehr.

Noor — Arabic word for light; the glow that brides get before marriage.

Porani — Pushto name for a shawl type of head covering.

Punjabi clothes — The Pushto name for Pakistani salwar kameez, dress consisting of a tunic and baggy pants.

Pushto — A language spoken in Afghanistan.

Qadr of Allah — The plan of God; one of the articles of Muslim belief, that everything happens within God's plan.

Quran — Muslim holy book.

Rakat — One unit of Muslim prayer.

Ruku — A position of prayer, when one bows with one's back parallel to the ground.

Salams — Greetings; short for Assalaamu alaikum.

Salwar — Baggy pants.

Shaitan — Satan; the devil.

Sheer payra — An Afghan sweet.

Subhanallah — An Arabic phrase meaning "Glory be to God," often said at times of shock/distress and at times of joy.

Sujud — Position of prostration in the Muslim prayers, where hands and knees are on the floor and the forehead and nose are touching the floor.

Sunnah — Extra prayers (not obligatory).

Surah Fatiha — The first chapter in the Quran. Literally "the opening." For Muslims this is similar in stature to the Lord's Prayer.

Tafseer — A detailed commentary and explanation, often in another language, of the Arabic text of the Quran.

Taliban — The name of an ultra-conservative section of Afghan
   society that took control of Afghanistan shortly after Russian
   withdrawal.

Tashakur — Pushto for thank you.

Ulema — Islamic scholars.

Walee — A woman's male guardian (father, brother, uncle, son)
   who looks out for her interests, especially during marriage
   ceremonies.

Wudu — Ritual washing performed before prayers.

Zuhr — Prayer performed right after high noon until just before
   mid-afternoon.

RUKHSANA KHAN is an award-winning author and story-teller. Born in Lahore, Pakistan, she is an expert on books with international and Muslim themes. She has presented at schools and communities across Canada and the US, as well as at the 2006 ALA Conference in New Orleans and the 2008 IBBY Congress in Denmark. Her books often feature Pakistan and the Middle East and include *The Roses in My Carpets*, *Many Windows*, *Silly Chicken* and *A New Life*. She has been shortlisted for the Ruth Schwartz Award and several readers' choice awards.

Rukhsana lives in Toronto with her family.